nobody does it better

a gossip girl novel

GEN
VON
(RS)

Gossip Girl novels by Cecily von Ziegesar:

nobody does it better

a gossip girl

novel

by

Cecily von Ziegesar

BLOOMSBURY

Published in Great Britain in 2005 by Bloomsbury Publishing Plc
36 Soho Square, London, W1D 3QY

This edition published by arrangement with
Little, Brown and Company (Inc.), New York, NY, USA
All rights reserved

 Produced by 17th Street Productions,
an Alloy, Inc. company
151 West 26th Street, New York, NY 10001, USA

A CIP catalogue record of this book is available from the British Library
ISBN 0 7475 7609 2
ISBN 9780747576099

All papers used by Bloomsbury Publishing are natural, recyclable
products made from wood grown in well-managed forests. The
manufacturing processes conform to the environmental regulations
of the country of origin.

Printed in Great Britain by Clays Ltd, St Ives plc

10 9 8 7 6 5

I must be cruel only to be kind.
　　　　　　　　　　　—William Shakespeare, *Hamlet*

 gossipgirl.co.uk

hey people!

Only two weeks left to make up our minds about which college we want to go to—for those of us who have a choice. Meanwhile, we are busy mastering the art of not flunking out of our last *ever* term of high school while spending as little time as possible actually in school or doing homework. If you see a group of immaculately groomed girls shedding their blue-and-white-seersucker school uniforms and lying out in Sheep Meadow in Central Park in their cute new Malia Mills bikinis, that's us. If you see a group of shirtless boys in rolled-up khakis and bare feet, platinum Cartier tank watches gleaming from their tanned, lacrosse-muscled arms, those would be our boyfriends. And okay, yeah, it's only 11 A.M. on a Friday and we're supposed to be in gym or AP French, but we're nearing the end of the most diffi-cult year of our lives and we have a lot of excess steam to blow off, so cut us some slack, okay?

Better yet, *join us.*

In case you've been hiding under a rock somewhere and don't yet know us—doesn't everyone?—we are the belles of the ball, the princesses and princes of New York's Upper East Side. Most of the time we live in penthouse apartments in those stately doorman build-ings on Park or Fifth Avenues or in town houses that take up half a city block. The rest of the time we're at one of our "country" houses, which vary in size and location from compounds in Connecticut or the Hamptons to medieval castles in Ireland to beachfront villas in St. Barts. Weekdays there is school—*yawn*—at one of Manhattan's small, single-sex, uniform-required private schools. Weekends we play *hard,* especially now that the weather is fine and our parents are off in their yachts or private jets or driver-operated town cars, leaving us crazy kids to do as we please.

And what pleases us most right now is one of our favorite three-letter words. You may not be doing it, but you're definitely talking about it. *Everyone's* talking about it. And some of us are doing it. Especially . . .

The couple that may as well be married

They sleep together, eat together, and have started sharing each other's clothes, as if they couldn't be bothered with sorting out the rumpled pile of his-and-hers clothing beside the bed and just shrugged into the nearest thing, knowing it would soon be shrugged off again. Neither of them can go anywhere alone without people asking "Where's ___?" as if it's totally unbelievable that they'd spend more than thirty seconds apart. I know, I can hear you scoffing already. Like, how boring to have only one boyfriend. But face it, they're definitely doing more than just *talking* about that three-letter word, which is more than can be said for the rest of us.

Your e-mail

Dear GG,
My dad is an independent film producer and he's at Cannes right now for the festival. Everyone is talking about this documentary about "privileged New York City teens," but no one knows who made it. First of all, are you in the film? Second of all, are you the one who made it?
—LAgirl

Dear LAgirl,
I can't really answer your first question because I haven't seen the film, but it sounds awfully familiar. . . . A certain shaven-headed girl *was* following everyone around with a camera a few weeks back. . . . As for your second question—I can barely take pictures with my camera-phone!
—GG

Sightings

S after midnight, tiptoeing out to the mailbox outside her **Fifth Avenue** apartment building with her arms full of big white envelopes emblazoned with various college crests. She was wearing an itty-bitty baby blue Cosabella nightgown that barely covered her famously gorgeous bottom (to the delight of all the doormen on duty and all the cabbies stuck in traffic), but tiptoed back inside again without mailing anything. It must be tough making a decision about next year when she got into every school she applied to, and maybe even some that she didn't! **C** taking his military-issue scary-looking black boots to **Tod's** for a little spruce-up. He's going to be the first cadet ever to wear pink tassels on his boots. **D** and **J** fighting over the mirror in **H&M**. Looks like a little sibling rivalry has set in now that they're both so famous. **V** at an Internet café in **Williamsburg** IMing random strangers. That girl has no fear. **K** and **I** feasting and scheming in **Jackson Hole**. Oh, God, what now? No sign of **N** or **B** . . . Jeez, don't they ever get bored of each other? What if they have to be apart next year?

Decisions, decisions . . . Where will we all be in one year's time? Can we possibly survive without each other? Try not to freak out—yet. You know where to find me in case you need help, or company, or want to invite me over for one of those spontaneous rooftop parties that end-of-the-year seniors are so famous for having.

You know I love you,

gossip girl

n's bedroom is 100% pure love

"Wake up!" Blair Waldorf yanked off the Black Watch plaid duvet and let it fall to the floor beside the antique sleigh bed. Nate Archibald lay sprawled across the mattress on his stomach, naked and very relaxed. Blair sat down beside him and bounced up and down as hard as she could. Nate kept his eyes closed as her ruthless bouncing jarred his golden brown head up and down. Why was it that s-e-x made her so *hyper* and him so *sleepy*?

"I'm awake," he mumbled. He opened one glittering green eye and instantly felt more awake than he had a second before. Blair was naked too, all five feet four inches of her, from her shiny coral-glossed toes to the chestnut brown waves of her grown-out pixie cut. She had the type of body that looked even better naked than in clothes. Soft without being fat, and more delicate than her usual costumes of preppy, neatly creased jeans and cashmere cardigans or short, tight little black dresses let on. She was still a pain in his ass, but they'd been in and out of love pretty much since they were eleven years old, and he'd wanted to get naked with her for even longer. How typical that it had taken Blair six and a half years to stop fighting with him and finally do it.

And once they'd done it, they couldn't *stop* doing it.

Nate reached up and pulled her down on top of him, kissing her randomly and ferociously because she was finally *his*, all his.

"Hey!" Blair giggled. The navy blue silk Roman blinds were raised and the windows were open, but it wasn't like she cared if anyone saw or heard them. They were in love, they were beautiful, and they were sex fiends. If anyone was looking, it was only because they were seriously jealous.

Besides, she relished the attention, even from the random perverted Peeping Toms and Thomasinas who happened to be spying on them through gold-plated opera glasses from the windows of the surrounding town houses.

They kissed for a while, but Nate was too worn out to do much else. Blair rolled away from him and lit a cigarette, giving Nate little puffs every once and a while like the actors in *Breathless*, the supercool black-and-white French film she'd watched earlier that day in AP French. The blond female lead always looked so chic and beautiful and was never without lipstick. All the people in the movie did all day was ride around on a Vespa motorbike, have sex, sit in cafés, and smoke. Of course they always looked gorgeous. But Blair had to keep her grades up if she wanted to get off Yale's wait list, and what with school and homework and sex with Nate every day after school, there was hardly time for primping. Blair's wavy brown hair was matted and sweaty, her lips were chapped from prolonged kissing and infrequent lip gloss application, and she hadn't plucked her eyebrows in two whole days. Not that she really minded. Sacrificing a little personal grooming time for sex was totally worth it. Besides, she'd read somewhere that an hour of sex burns three hundred and sixty calories, so even if she was a little scruffy, at least she'd be skinny!

She reached up and felt the stubble gathering between her dark, neatly arched eyebrows. Okay, so maybe she minded just a *teensy* bit, but she could always grab a cab down to Elizabeth Arden for an eyebrow wax.

Stubble aside, Blair had never felt so happy. After finally doing it with Nate nearly two weeks ago, she was a whole new woman. The only dark cloud in her rosy sky was the irritating fact that she was still only wait-listed at Yale. Just exactly how were she and Nate going to get together every afternoon if she wound up having to go to Georgetown in DC—the only school that had actually accepted her—and he was up at Yale in New Haven, Connecticut, or Brown in Providence, Rhode Island, or one of the other great schools he'd so unfairly gotten into? Not that she was bitter, but Nate had shown up stoned for the SATs, took no APs, and barely had a B average, while she was in every AP Constance Billard offered, had gotten a 1490 on her SAT, and had almost an A+ average.

Okay, so maybe she was *slightly* bitter.

"If I joined the Peace Corps and spent a couple of years building sewers and making sandwiches for starving children in, like, Rio or somewhere, then Yale would *have* to take me, wouldn't they?" she asked aloud.

Nate grinned. Here was the thing about Blair that he loved. She was spoiled, but she wasn't lazy. She knew what she wanted, and because she believed absolutely that she could have *everything* she wanted if she tried hard enough to get it, she never stopped trying.

"I heard everyone gets sick in the Peace Corps. And you have to speak the native language."

"I'll do it in France then." Blair blew smoke up at the ceiling. "Or one of those African countries where they speak French." She tried to imagine herself conversing with the natives in some arid African village while balancing a clay pot of fresh goat's milk on her head and wearing an elaborately dyed caftan that could be supremely sexy if tied in the right places. She'd have a killer tan and would be nothing but muscle and bone from all the hard work and horrible intestinal diseases. Children would clamor at her knees for the Godiva chocolates she'd order for them, and she'd smile serenely down at them like a beautiful, unwrinkled Mother Teresa. When she returned to the States she'd win some Peace Corps award for best volunteer, or even the Nobel Peace Prize. She'd have dinner with the president, who would write her a recommendation to Yale, and then Yale would fall all over themselves to accept her.

Nate was pretty sure the Peace Corps only helped out in third-world countries, not economically thriving places like France, and no way would Blair last more than half an hour in some remote African village where they didn't have Sephora or even flushing toilets. Poor Blair. It was completely unfair that he'd gotten into Yale without really trying, while she, who'd wanted to go to Yale since she was two years old, had been wait-listed. Then again, Nate was used to getting things without really trying.

He propped his head up on his hand and tenderly smoothed Blair's dark hair away from her forehead. "Unless you hear soon that you got in, I promise I won't go to Yale," he vowed. "I'm fine with going to Brown or wherever."

"Really?" Blair stamped out her cigarette in the sailboat-shaped marble ashtray beside Nate's bed and flung her arms around his neck. Nate was by far the best boyfriend a girl could ever ask for. She couldn't imagine why she'd ever broken up with him, not once, but again and again.

Because he cheated on her again and again?

All Blair knew now was that she never ever wanted to leave Nate's side. She rested her cheek against his strong, bare chest. Now that she thought about it, moving into the Archibalds' town house wasn't such a bad idea, since her own house wasn't exactly an episode of *Seventh Heaven* right now. Her mother had given birth to her baby sister just over two weeks ago and was now suffering from severe postpartum depression. Just this morning Blair had left her mother weeping over a DVD sent from a Peruvian Alpaca farm. Apparently, if you adopted a herd of alpaca yearlings, you could custom-order handwoven blankets and sweaters made from the hair of the animals in your herd. Her baby sister would soon be the proud new owner of a hairy white alpaca blanket that would be completely useless all summer long, and probably the rest of her life, unless as a teenager she got into the hippie handmade-chic thing, cut a head-hole into the blanket, and fashioned it into a poncho.

Back when her mother was still pregnant, she had asked Blair to name the baby, and out of devotion to her favorite college Blair had chosen the name Yale. Now baby Yale served as a living, breathing, very noisy reminder that no matter how stunning Blair's record was, the school had all but rejected her. Worse still, the baby had taken over her bedroom, and she was forced to sleep in her stepbrother Aaron's room until she left for school in the fall. Aaron was a vegan Rastafarian dog-lover, so the room had been decorated specifically for him in wall-to-wall organic, environmentally sound products in shades of eggplant and wild sage. To add insult to injury, Blair's cat, Kitty Minky, had taken to peeing on the barley husk cushions and throwing up on the woven sea grass floor mats in an effort to rid the room of the scent of Aaron's dog, a drooling boxer named Mookie.

Hello, nasty?

Move in with Nate. Blair didn't know why she hadn't thought of it before. A freaky mother, a cat-pee-soaked bedroom, and a newborn baby sister named Yale were not exactly conducive to studying or s-e-x. It was only natural for her to seek other accommodation. Of course there was always Serena's house, but they'd tried that before and wound up fighting. Besides, Serena couldn't offer her much in the way of s-e-x.

Unless those old rumors were actually true . . .

Nate ran his hands lazily up and down her smooth bare back. "Have you ever thought about getting a tattoo?" he asked out of nowhere as he traced the lines of her shoulder blades.

Except for a brief stint in rehab earlier that year, Nate had been stoned pretty much all day every day since he was eleven, and Blair was used to his random questions. She wrinkled her pointy, slightly upturned nose at the thought of having a big scar filled with black ink. "Gross," she responded. Leave that to skanky-looking actresses like Angelina Jolie.

Nate shrugged. He'd always thought carefully chosen, tiny tattoos in just the right places were insanely sexy. A little black cat between Blair's shoulder blades, for instance, would totally suit her. But before he had a chance to take the notion any further, Blair briskly changed the subject.

"Nate?" She nuzzled her face into his manly, perfect collarbone. "Do you think your parents would mind if I stayed—?" Before she could finish her sentence, the downstairs buzzer rang.

Nate's personal wing of the town house took up the entire top floor, necessitating his very own front door buzzer.

He rolled away from Blair and swung his feet to the floor.

"Yeah?" he called, pressing the button on the intercom.

"Delivery!" Jeremy Scott Tompkinson shouted in his hoarse stoner voice. "Hurry while it's still hot!"

Nate heard laughter and other voices in the background. Blair waited for him to tell them to get lost. Instead, he pressed the button to unlock the door and let them in.

"I should get dressed," Blair observed tersely. She slid out of bed and stomped into Nate's adjoining bathroom. How could he be smart enough to get into Yale, yet too dumb to understand that inviting his stoner friends up to their steamy love den would totally ruin the mood?

Not that Yale had accepted Nate because of his smarts: the school needed a few good lacrosse players. End of story.

At least Blair had an excuse to use the delicious L'Occitane sandalwood body shampoo the housekeeper stocked in Nate's shower. She toweled herself off with a thick navy blue Ralph Lauren towel, slipped on her flimsy pink silk Cosabella underwear, zipped up her blue-and-white-seer-sucker Constance Billard School spring uniform skirt, and buttoned two of the six buttons on her white linen Calvin Klein three-quarter-sleeve blouse. Braless and barefoot, it was the perfect my-girlfriend-just-got-out-of-the-shower-and-would-you-please-leave? look. Hopefully Nate's friends would get the hint, make like bees, and fuck off. She tousled her damp hair with her fingers and pushed open the bathroom door.

"Bonjour!" A buxom, raven-haired, long-legged L'École girl greeted Blair from Nate's bed. Blair had met the girl before at parties. Her name was Lexus or Lexique or something equally annoying, a sixteen-year-old junior who'd done some modeling as a child in Paris and was now working on perfecting the French hippie-slut look. Lexique, whose name was really Lexie, was wearing a lavender-and-mustard-yellow hand-dyed cotton wraparound dress that looked homemade but had actually been purchased at Kirna Zabete for four hundred and fifty dollars, and those ugly flat Pakistani sheep-herder sandals from Barneys that everyone but Blair seemed to think were so cool this year. Lexie's face was makeup-free, and she cradled an acoustic guitar in her skinny arms. On the bed beside her was a Ziploc bag full of pot.

What a rebel. Most L'École girls never go anywhere without a pack of Gitanes, red lipstick, and heels.

"The boys are making bong hits on the roof," Lexie explained. She strummed her thumb across the guitar strings. "*Alors,* want to jam with me till they get back?"

Jam?

Blair wrinkled her nose with even more emphasis than she had at the thought of getting a tattoo. She was *so* not into the whole getting-high, playing-guitars-and-laughing-at-your-friends'-totally-stupid-stoned-observations scene, and she really didn't want to hang out with this Lexique girl, who obviously thought she was the coolest French girl in New York. She'd rather watch *Oprah* reruns on Oxygen in her cat-pee-soaked room while her delusional mom wept over baby alpacas.

Someone had stuck a stick of burning amber incense into the cork heel of one of Blair's new mint green Christian Dior espadrilles. She grabbed the stick of incense and jammed it into a porthole in one of Nate's beloved model sailboats on his desk. Then she laced up her shoes, buttoned a few more buttons on her blouse, and grabbed her vintage Gucci bamboo-handled tote bag. "Please tell Nathaniel that I've gone home," she instructed briskly.

"Peace!" Lexie saluted Blair with stoned gaiety. *"Au revoir!"* A tattoo of the sun, moon, and stars was printed on her shoulder blade.

Hence Nate's sudden interest in tattoos?

Blair stomped down the stairs and let herself out onto Eighty-second Street. It felt like summer already. The sun was still two hours from setting, and the air smelled of fresh-cut grass from nearby Central Park, and suntan lotion from all the half-naked girls hurrying home to their apartments on Park Avenue. A gaggle of eleventh-grade St. Jude's Nate-and-Jeremy-wannabes were hovering around the downstairs buzzer outside Nate's town house. One of them had a guitar slung over his shoulder.

"Bien sûr. Come on up!" Blair heard Lexie call out to them over the intercom, as if she lived there.

Nate's house seemed to draw all the stoner kids on the Upper East Side with some sort of spiritual magnetic pull. And Blair swore she didn't mind—really, she didn't—as long as she didn't have to sit around watching them all *jam.* After all she and Nate had been though, Blair knew it was going to be different this time. She and Nate were together spiritually, and now physically, too, which meant she could leave him alone, feeling perfectly confident that he wouldn't dream of cheating on her.

She carried on down Eighty-second street toward Fifth Avenue, checking her cell phone for a message from Nate at every corner. Obviously he'd call any second now. Like all possessive, aggressive, obsessive girls, she liked to think Nate didn't have a life without her.

Then again, if he didn't, she'd go completely nuts.

little diva gives big diva some sound advice

"They gave us five spreads," Serena van der Woodsen explained as she flipped through the hot-off-the-press June issue of *W* magazine. "That's ten whole pages!" The world-famous fashion designer Les Best had just messengered the fashion magazine over to her apartment with a note that read, *"As ever, you are fabulous, darling. And so's that dark-haired little hottie friend of yours!"*

The same supposed dark-haired little hottie, fourteen-year-old Jenny Humphrey, was desperately trying not to pee in her pants. Serena, the coolest senior girl at Constance Billard, and totally famous and beautiful model/Upper East Side girl-about-town, had actually asked *her* to hang out after school today. She was now sitting in Serena's huge, awesomely old-fashioned bedroom—her private sanctuary—*on her bed*, flipping through the latest issue of the coolest fashion magazine in the world, looking for pages featuring *the two of them* modeling the type of amazing designer clothes Jenny had always gazed at longingly in stores but never once dreamed she'd actually wear. It was so unreal she could hardly breathe.

"Here, look!" Serena squealed, stabbing at the page with a long, slender finger. "Don't we look like badasses?!"

Jenny leaned in closer to see, happily inhaling the sweet scent of Serena's custom-blended patchouli oil perfume. Across Serena's perfect lap lay a spread of the two girls dressed head-to-toe in Les Best couture, motoring down the beach in a dune buggy, the Ferris wheel at Coney Island rising up behind them, all lit up. The style of the picture was typical Jonathan Joyce—the über-famous fashion photographer who had shot the spread—totally natural and unposed, like he'd just happened upon these two girls riding their dune buggy on the beach at sunset and having the time of their lives. Indeed they did look like badasses in their crazy turquoise-and-black-striped leggings, turquoise leather vests over white bikini tops, and white leather knee-high go-go boots with teeny-tiny heels. Their hair was winged back, their nails were painted white, their lips were painted cotton candy pink, and peacock feathers dangled from their ears. It was all very retro eighties/futuristic/cutting edge, and absurdly cool.

Jenny couldn't pull her eyes away. There she was, *in a magazine*, and for the first time ever her enormous chest wasn't the focal point of the picture. In fact the two girls looked so fresh and pure the picture was almost *wholesome*. It was beyond what Jenny could have hoped for. It was heavenly.

"I love the look on your face," Serena observed. "It's like you've just been kissed or something."

Jenny giggled, feeling very much like she *had* just been kissed. "You look pretty too."

Oops, look who has a major crush on Serena—just like everyone else in the universe!

But Jenny's crush was deeper than most: she actually wanted to *be* Serena. And the thing Serena had that she still lacked was a questionable past—that alluring air of mystery.

"Bet it seems like forever ago that you were kicked out of boarding school," Jenny ventured boldly, her eyes fixed on the magazine.

"I was worried I'd never get into a single college because of all that," Serena sighed. "If I'd known I'd get into all of them, I'd never have applied to so many schools."

Poor thing. If only we all had that problem.

"Did you like boarding school?" Jenny persisted, turning to gaze up at Serena with her big brown eyes. "I mean, more than going to school in the city?"

Serena lay back on the four-poster bed and stared up at the white eyelet canopy overhead. She'd been eight years old when she'd first gotten the bed, and she'd felt like a little princess every night when she'd gone to sleep. As a matter of fact, she still felt like a princess, only bigger.

"I loved feeling like I had my own life, apart from my parents and the friends I'd known practically since I was born. I liked going to school with boys, and eating with them in the dining hall. It was like having a whole class of brothers. But I missed my room and the city, and weekends hanging out." She pulled off her white cotton socks and threw them across the room. "And I know it sounds totally spoiled, but I missed having a maid."

Jenny nodded. She liked the sound of eating in a dining hall with a whole bunch of boys. She liked it a lot. And she'd never had a maid, so it wasn't as if she'd miss that.

"I guess it was good preparation for college," Serena mused. "I mean, if I actually decide to *go* to college."

Jenny closed the magazine and held it against her chest. "I thought you were going to Brown."

Serena pulled a down-feather pillow over her face and then pulled it off again. Was it really necessary to answer so many questions? All of a sudden she kind of wished she hadn't invited Jenny over. "I don't know where I'm going. I might not even go. I don't know," she mumbled, tossing the pillow on the floor next to her socks. Her flaxen hair fanned out around her perfectly chiseled face as she gazed skyward with her enormous blue eyes. She looked so lovely, Jenny half expected a flock of white doves to flap out from underneath the bed.

Serena grabbed the stereo remote from off her bedside table and clicked on the old Raves CD that she'd been listening to a lot lately. The CD had come out last summer and reminded her of a time when she was completely carefree. She hadn't been kicked out of boarding school yet. She hadn't thought about applying to college. She hadn't even started modeling yet.

"What's so great about Brown?" she questioned aloud, although her brother Erik went there and would be totally pissed off if she decided not to go. Plus, she'd met a hunky Latin painter at Brown who was still totally in love with her. But what about Harvard, and that sensitive, nearsighted tour guide who'd also fallen in love with her? Or Yale and the Whiffenpoofs, who'd written a song for her? And there was always Princeton, which she hadn't even visited. After all, it was the closest to the city. "Maybe I should just defer for a year or two, get my own apartment. Model some, and maybe try acting."

"Or you could do both. Like Claire Danes," Jenny suggested. "I mean, once you stop going to school, it's probably really hard to go back."

As if you'd know, Little Miss Helpful.

Serena rolled off the bed and stood in front of the full-length mirror that hung on the back of her closet door. She'd rumpled her turquoise Marni peasant blouse, and her blue-and-white-seersucker Constance Billard uniform was hanging lopsidedly on her hips. That morning she'd been late as usual and had tripped running to school, losing her orange Miu Miu cork-heeled clogs and landing facedown on the sidewalk. Now the iridescent pink polish on the big toe of her left foot was chipped, and a purple-and-yellow bruise stood out on her right knee.

"What a mess," she complained.

Jenny wasn't sure how Serena could even stand to look at herself in the mirror every day without passing out in amazement at her own perfection. That anyone as perfect as Serena could have *issues* was totally unfathomable. "I'm sure you'll figure it out," she told the older girl, becoming suddenly distracted by a photo of Erik van der Woodsen, Serena's hot older brother, propped up on Serena's bedside table in a silver Tiffany frame. Tall and lanky, with the same pale blond hair, cut in a long shag framing his face, Erik was a male version of Serena. Same huge dark blue eyes, same full mouth that turned up at the corners, same straight white teeth and aristocratic chin. In the picture he was standing on a rocky beach, tan and shirtless. Jenny squeezed her bare knees together. Those chest muscles, that stomach, those arms—oh! If boarding school was filled with boys who were even half as gorgeous as Erik van der Woodsen, they could sign her up!

Easy there, cowgirl.

Serena's pink iMac beeped, indicating that she had just received e-mail.

"Probably one of our fans," Serena joked, although Jenny thought she was serious. Serena went over to her antique letter-writing desk, jiggled her mouse, and clicked on the latest e-mail message.

Dear Serena,
Our sorority totally worships Les Best and
some of us were at his New York show this
spring, so you can imagine how completely
thrilled we were when we heard you were
considering attending Princeton this fall.
And if you do go to Princeton, you have to
become a Tri Delt. We already have all
these amazing fundraising ideas for this
year, including a Les Best fashion show to
benefit the Wild Horses of Chincoteague,
featuring us, the Tri Delts, as models!
The best part is you won't even have to
pledge. Congratulations, Serena, you're
already a sister! All you have to do now
is get your behind up to Princeton a few
days early this August so you can get a
good room in our house.
We totally can't wait. Big kisses.

Your sis,
Sheri

Serena read the message again and then logged off, staring
at the blank screen in shock. Pushy sorority sisters were just
about the last people she wanted to hear from, and anyway,
wasn't Princeton supposed to be sort of *intellectual*? She
picked up the phone to call Blair and then slammed it down
again, realizing she'd completely forgotten that Jenny was

even there. Jenny was sweet and adorable and everything—but didn't she have, like, homework or a movie to go to or something?

See, even perfect goddesses have a bitchy side.

Jenny slid off the bed and hitched up her extrawide supportive bra straps, guessing that she was about to be dismissed. "You know, my brother Dan is singing for the Raves now," she announced. "His first gig with them is tomorrow night. I can put you on the special guest list if you want to come."

Jenny wasn't even sure if there was a special guest list. All she knew was she was getting in free because she was Dan's sister. Dan thought he was so famous now that he was a member of a band with the number one album on the East Coast, but if she showed up at the gig with Serena—two gorgeous models out on the town in matching Les Best dresses—she'd completely outfamous him.

Serena wrinkled her nose. She wanted to go to the Raves gig, she really did, but she and her parents had already RVSPed yes to some Yale prospective students' get-to-know-you party tomorrow night. She couldn't exactly make her parents go by themselves.

"I don't think I can," she explained apologetically. "There's this Yale thing I have to go to. But I'll try to get down there if it finishes early."

Jenny nodded and stuffed the issue of *W* into her Gap tote bag, disappointed. She'd envisioned making an entrance at the Lower East Side club with Serena. Never mind the Raves—they were rock stars, big deal. She and Serena were supermodels—at least Serena was. Heads were guaranteed to turn.

Guess she'll just have to satisfy herself with being the lead singer's little sister. Like that would ever be enough.

talk about an identity crisis

"Crack me like an *egg*!"

Daniel Humphrey glared at himself in his bedroom mirror and took a long drag on a half-smoked Camel. A lame-voiced wimp in worn, khaki-colored corduroys and a maroon Gap T-shirt. Not exactly rock 'n' roll.

"Crack me like an *egg*!" he wailed again, trying to look angst-ridden, rebellious, and sickly cool all at the same time. The problem was, his voice always broke when he went into the higher ranges, coming out in a breathy whisper, and his face looked soft and young and totally unthreatening.

Dan rubbed at his bony chin and thought about growing a goatee. Vanessa had always had a strong aversion to facial hair, but what she thought was no longer relevant now that they were no longer a couple.

Almost two weeks ago at Vanessa's eighteenth birthday party at her apartment in Williamsburg, Brooklyn, Dan had been discovered by the megapopular indie band the Raves. Or rather, his *poems* had been. Thinking they would both go to NYU next year and live happily ever after, Dan had moved in with Vanessa only a few days before. But their relationship had quickly deteriorated. More depressed than usual, Dan had been sitting in a corner during the party, chugging Grey Goose vodka straight out of the bottle. Meanwhile, the Raves showed up at the party and their lead guitarist, Damian Polk, stumbled upon a stack of black notebooks filled with Dan's poetry. Damian and his band members had gone crazy over the poems, insisting they'd work perfectly as lyrics. Their lead singer had just mysteriously quit—*rehab anyone?*—and so they decided to ask Dan to be their front man. By then Dan was piss drunk and thought the whole thing was totally hilarious. Throwing himself into the task with drunken fervor, he'd stolen the show, electrifying drunken partiers with his brazen performance.

He'd thought it was a one-time deal, a way of distracting himself from the fact that he'd just broken up with the only girl who'd ever loved him. The next day he discovered that he was a card-carrying member of the band, and completely in over his head.

During rehearsals Dan found that his normally sober self was physically incapable of putting out the same reckless energy that he'd had at the party, and, compared to the other band members, who were all in their twenties and wore clothes tailor-made for them by avant-garde designers like Pistolcock and Better Than Naked, he felt like a geeky, squeaky little kid. He'd even asked Damian Polk why in hell the Raves wanted him to be their lead singer in the first place. Damian had replied simply, "It's all about the words, man."

Dude, just because he could write didn't mean he could *sing*. But maybe if he *looked* more like he could sing, he might actually convince people that he deserved to be in the band.

Dan shuffled through his messy desk drawers searching for the battery-operated beard trimmer he'd bought last year during a week of experimenting with the length of his sideburns. He moved on to his little sister Jenny's room, and finally found it under her bed, inexplicably rolled up inside an old pink bath towel.

Little sister lesson number one: If you want to keep your shit, put a padlock on your door.

Not bothering to return to his own room, he went over to the mirror on the back of Jenny's closet door and tugged at the outgrown Mr. Trendy Artiste haircut he'd gotten soon after one of his poems was published in the *New Yorker*. Now that he'd made the switch from bohemian poet to gritty rock star, it was time for a change.

Eek! Doesn't *everyone* know not to try a new look the day before a big event?

The trimmer buzzed to life and Dan began shaving the back of his neck, watching the light brown strands gather on the faded chocolate-colored carpet in mousy clumps. Then he stopped, worried all of a sudden that a beard trimmer didn't have exactly the right sort of blades to shave one's entire head with. It might leave weird red track marks all over his skull, or shave his head unevenly so that it looked like his hair had been *eaten* rather than cut.

Sure he wanted to look hard-core, but not chewed-head hard-core.

He debated whether or not to continue. If he stopped now, the shaved parts would be completely concealed by the rest of his hair until he bent over, and then, voilà—a shaved neck. It was kind of cool knowing the shaved part was there without being able to see it. Then again, an unnoticeable haircut wasn't exactly the look he was going for.

He put the beard trimmer down, propped a Camel between his lips, and reached for Jenny's phone. If there was one person who knew anything about shaving heads, it was

Vanessa. She'd kept her own head shaved since ninth grade, and, shunning the expensive salons like Frederic Fekkai and Elizabeth Arden's Red Door that her coiffed classmates frequented, insisted on shaving it herself. Secretly he'd always thought she look prettier with a little more hair, but since she obviously thought she looked great bald, he wasn't about to say anything.

"If this is about the apartment-share, I will be calling you once I've reviewed your online application," Vanessa said robotically when she picked up.

"Hey, it's me, Dan," Dan responded brightly. "What's up?"

Vanessa didn't answer right away. She'd wanted to give Dan space to grow and blossom into the next Kurt Cobain or John Keats or whatever the fuck he wanted to be, but breaking up and kicking him out of her apartment hadn't exactly been easy for her. The casual let's-just-be-friends tone in Dan's voice made her heart feel like a deflated balloon.

"I'm kind of busy actually." She typed a bunch of nonsense into her computer to make it sound like she was drastically preoccupied. "I have a lot of applications to go through—for the new roommate—you know?"

"Oh." Dan hadn't been aware that Vanessa was looking for a roommate. Then again, with her older sister Ruby gone on tour with her band, it would be kind of lonely and boring living all alone in the apartment, especially without him to keep her company.

For a fleeting moment Dan was so overcome with regret he felt like grabbing a pen and writing a tragic breakup poem using the words *cut* or *shaved*, but then his newly shorn neck began to burn and prickle, and he remembered why he'd called Vanessa in the first place.

"I just had a quick question." He took several quick puffs

on his cigarette and then absentmindedly dropped it into a vase of daisies wilting on Jenny's desk. "You know when you shave your head? Is there like, a certain kind of razor you use? Like a certain blade?"

Vanessa's first impulse was to warn him that with a shaved head he'd look like a skinny seven-year-old leukemia patient who'd just been through chemo, but she was tired of protecting him from his own mistakes, especially now that they were "just friends." "Wahl blade number ten. Look, I gotta go."

Dan picked up his beard trimmer. It was from CVS and didn't have a blade size. Maybe he'd be better off going to a barber. "Okay. I'll see you at my gig tomorrow night though, right?"

"Maybe," Vanessa replied breezily. "If I get this roommate thing figured out. Gotta go. 'Bye!"

Dan hung up and picked up the beard trimmer once more. "Crack me like an egg!" he shouted, holding it in front of his chin like a microphone. He whipped off his T-shirt and stuck out his pale, skinny gut, trying to look saucily bored and rebellious, like a shorter, thinner, less-fucked-up Jim Morrison. "Crack me like an egg!" he wailed, falling on his knees.

His dad, Rufus, suddenly appeared in the doorway, wearing a cigarette-burned gray Old Navy sweatshirt and the pink terrycloth headband Jenny used to keep her hair back when she washed her face. "Good thing your sister's too busy to hang out with us after school anymore. She might not be too thrilled to find you stripping in her room," he commented.

"I'm rehearsing." Dan rose to his feet with as much dignity as he could muster. "Do you mind?"

"Go right ahead." Rufus stood in the doorway, scratching his chest and fingering the unfiltered Camel tucked behind his left ear. He was a work-at-home single dad, the editor of lesser-known Beat poets and esoteric writers no one had ever heard of. "I think if you put the emphasis on every *other* word, it might be more effective."

Dan cocked his head and handed Rufus the beard trimmer. "Show me."

Rufus grinned. "Okay, but I'm not taking my shirt off."

Thank the Lord.

He held the beard trimmer away from his face, as if worried that it might turn on by itself and buzz off his famously unkempt beard. "Crack *me* like an *egg*!" he howled, his brown eyes gleaming. He handed back the trimmer. "Try it."

Of course Dan's dad had sounded just exactly the way Dan wanted to sound. He tossed the trimmer onto Jenny's bed and pulled his shirt back on. "I have homework to do," he grumbled.

Rufus shrugged his shoulders. "Okay, I'll leave you alone." He winked at his son. "Decided where you want to go next year yet?"

"No," Dan answered hollowly, then shuffled out of Jenny's room and back to his own. His dad was so gung-ho about the whole college thing, it was seriously annoying.

"Columbia's close!" Rufus called after him. "You could live at home!"

As if he hadn't already mentioned that a thousand times.

Alone in his room, Dan found a rubber band in his desk drawer and tied his hair up into a stubby ponytail, leaving the shaved part exposed. He picked up the beard trimmers again. "Crack *me* like an *egg*!" he whispered, imitating his father as best he could. He grimaced. There just wasn't enough gristle in his voice to sound convincing.

Trading the trimmer for the pile of college catalogs he'd

been thumbing through for the past three months, he flopped down on his bed. Only one more week to choose between NYU, Brown, Colby, or Evergreen. He flipped to a picture of a tweedy, intellectual-looking Brown student, his back propped against the trunk of a giant elm tree, scribbling away in a notebook like a young Keats. He looked exactly as Dan had envisioned he'd look himself next year—before he'd been discovered by the Raves and before he'd just shaved the back of his head.

He ran his finger over the shaved part of his head and glanced down at his outfit. He'd have to go shopping, because none of his clothes went with his hair anymore.

And you thought that was something only girls worry about.

If only Jenny were there to help out, Dan thought grimly. But his little sister was too busy being a supermodel to go through his closet with him and tell him what was lame and what was acceptable. Dan picked up a cup of Folgers instant coffee that had been cooling on the floor since that morning and took a sip. He grimaced at his reflection in the mirror, and for an instant he could almost envision himself up on stage, giving the audience the same annoyed, pissed-off grimace. Maybe, just *maybe* he could pull this off, without even his sister's help.

Or maybe not.

v takes the room out of roommate

Fireeater: i keep a pretty sick schedule, like i sleep all day and work at night.

Hairlesskat: what do you do?

Fireeater: duh, i'm a performer

Hairlesskat: you really eat fire?

Fireeater: i'm working on it. mostly i dance with my snakes.

Hairlesskat: snakes?

Fireeater: yeah i have four snakes.

Fireeater: you're okay with pets right?

Fireeater: you still there?

Fireeater: yo, hello?

"Nice try, loser!" Vanessa Abrams logged off her computer and went over to her closet. She'd taken off her hot and hideous maroon wool Constance Billard School winter uniform—the only uniform she owned—two hours ago and hadn't bothered to change into anything else. Even though the girl Vanessa was supposed to interview in three minutes had sounded cool in her e-mail that morning, she probably wouldn't be too psyched if Vanessa greeted her at the door in her black cotton Hanes underwear. Vanessa pulled a folded pair of pants off the top shelf in her bedroom closet without even looking. Everything in her closet was black, and she was a strong believer in shopping in duplicate. If you owned six pairs of straight-legged black stretch Levis, you never really had to think about what you were going to wear, and you only had to do laundry once a week. She pulled the jeans up around her pale and slightly pudgy hips, yanked her black long-sleeved V-neck tee down over them, and ran her hands over her shaved, dark head. She might have looked odd to all the so-called "normal" girls she went to school with, but the girl she was about to meet sounded more interesting than they could ever hope to be—well, at least she had online.

The downstairs buzzer rang, just as she'd anticipated. Vanessa went over to the window and pulled aside the curtain, which was really just a black poly-blend Martha Stewart Everyday bedsheet she and her sister Ruby had bought at Kmart last Halloween. On the street two floors below, a drunk homeless guy was shouting at empty parked cars. A little boy with green spiked hair and no shirt on sped down the sidewalk on a mountain bike that was way too big for him. The crumbling cement block that served as Vanessa's front stoop was empty. The prospective roommate was already on her way up.

"Please be normal," Vanessa murmured. Not that she actually liked normal girls. Normal girls, like the girls in her class at Constance, wore pink lip gloss and different versions of the exact same pair of shoes and were religious about things like highlights and pedicures. In her e-mail application this girl Beverly had said she was an art student at Pratt, so she was older, for one thing, and was probably kind of alternative. Hopefully she'd be as cool as she sounded.

Vanessa opened the door to the apartment just as Beverly mounted the top of the stairs. And to Vanessa's complete surprise, Beverly wasn't a she, she was a *he*.

Vanessa had sort of forgotten to specify that she was looking for a *girl* roommate in her Web posting.

A deliberate mistake?

"Bet you thought I was female, right?" Beverly asked, extending his hand for Vanessa to shake. "The name is totally old-fashioned and totally misleading. Don't worry, I'm used to it."

Vanessa tried not to look surprised, which wasn't hard for her. She'd mastered the unexpressive stare long ago while eating alone day after day in the Constance Billard School cafeteria, tuning out the senseless babble of her beautiful, bitchy classmates. She tucked her fingers into the back pockets of her jeans and nonchalantly led the way into the apartment. "I was just IMing with this weirdo chick who dances with snakes. You don't have any snakes, do you?"

"Nope." Beverly pressed his palms together in praying position and surveyed the starkly decorated apartment. The walls were white and the wood floors were bare. The kitchen was tiny and opened onto the living room/second bedroom, which was furnished with a futon and a TV. The only decorations were framed stills from the dark, morose films that Vanessa notoriously made in her spare time.

"Whose work?" Beverly asked, gesturing at a black-and-white photograph of a pigeon pecking at a used condom in Madison Square Park.

Vanessa discovered she was staring at Beverly's firm, round buttocks and quickly averted her eyes. "Mine," she replied hoarsely. "It's from a film I made earlier this year."

Beverly nodded his head, keeping his palms pressed

together as he examined the other photographs. Vanessa loved that he didn't start babbling about how offbeat or depressing they were, the way people usually did. Just the way he'd said, "Whose work?" made her feel like a real artist.

"Would you like a beer?" she asked. Her fridge was uncharacteristically full of beer from her insane eighteenth-birthday party two weekends ago, and she'd take any opportunity to get rid of it. "Sorry, I don't have much else except water."

"Water would be fine," Beverly replied, and Vanessa found herself liking him even more. Ask any high-school boy if he wanted a beer and he'd down a whole six-pack in three seconds flat. All Beverly needed was a little water to whet his palate, and a place to live—for instance, *with her*.

Whoa . . . Slow down, Nellie! What about the interview?

Vanessa went into the tiny open kitchen and got out a vintage Scooby-Doo glass and some ice and a pitcher of filtered water from the refrigerator. She filled the glass slowly, surreptitiously studying Beverly as she did so. His small, intense eyes were pale blue, and his short, tousled hair was nearly black. The palms of his hands and his fingernails were stained black with some sort of ink he must have been using in his artwork, and his drab green T-shirt was flecked with what looked like sawdust. His black pants were just the sort of loose black cotton poplin slacks she would have worn every day if she were a guy, and on his feet were a pair of those thin orange rubber flip-flops you can buy at the drugstore for ninety-nine cents. He was so not like the people she went to school with, Vanessa couldn't help but feel kind of excited.

Could that have anything to do with the fact that he's a guy?

She walked around the counter and handed Beverly the

water, already envisioning what it would be like to stay up late and watch movies together. She could bring him water and he would nod his head at her in that thoughtful, sexy way of his. And then they'd begin to dissect Stanley Kubrick's work, film by film . . . *naked.*

Vanessa took a seat on the futon sofa and Beverly sat down beside her.

"So, I'm kind of between places right now," he explained. "I was in a dorm and now I'm in this group work-live arrangement with a bunch of artists in this warehouse space down by the Brooklyn Navy Yard. It can get pretty crazy there sometimes, though." He chuckled. "I just need a place to crash where I don't have to worry about my fingers getting hacked off while I'm sleeping—you know, for someone's 'body parts' sculpture or something?"

Vanessa nodded happily. She knew exactly how he felt.

Really?

Of course, she'd never expected to share an apartment with a *guy*—other than Dan—but she was eighteen now, an adult, able to make her own decisions and mature enough to have a guy roommate and no intention of jumping his bones.

Right.

"The thing is," Beverly continued, "it would be kind of weird living with someone I'd never even breathed the same air with before, you know?"

Vanessa's big brown eyes widened. So he *didn't* want to live with her? "I guess so," she responded glumly.

"I wondered if maybe we could like, hang out for a few weeks first. Do stuff. Get to know each other. See if it could work out," he added.

Vanessa sat on her hands, feeling embarrassingly like one of those so-called normal girls she hated after some hottie had asked them to a prom or whatever they called those ridiculous dress-up parties they were always going to because it gave them the opportunity to buy a new dress. Beverly *did* want to live with her. He just wanted to get to know her first. How refreshing and exciting to finally meet someone so intelligent, creative, cool—and *hot*!

"Well, I *am* interviewing other people," she responded, not wanting to appear too eager. "But that sounds like a good idea. I mean, you're right. It's important to know who you're about to move in with."

"Exactly." Beverly polished off the water, stood up, and carried the glass over to the sink.

Wow, he even cleans up after himself.

He flip-flopped back into the living room. "We could do something this weekend or—"

Suddenly Vanessa had an idea. What better way to show Dan that she'd moved on and had a life of her own beyond him and his selfish self than to bring a guy to his first gig? "Actually, an old friend of mine is singing with the Raves tomorrow night. Want to go?"

Thankfully Beverly was mature enough not to jump up and down and freak out about the fact that she knew someone who sang with the Raves. He pressed his palms together and nodded his head in that sexy, monklike way of his. "Sure. I'll call you tomorrow to make a plan."

Vanessa walked him to the door and then rushed to the window, following his nice ass with her eyes as he flip-flopped his way down South Sixth Street and then disappeared into the maze of old factory warehouses that made up Williamsburg's landscape. Saturday mornings she and Beverly would sit by that very window, making use of its southern exposure to make their art. He would work silently at his canvas, smearing black ink all over it with his hands while she filmed him. And both of them would be . . . *naked*.

Of course.

How exciting to live with an artist. Of course, Dan was a poet, but that was different. All he did was scribble in notebooks all day, drinking bad coffee and getting shakier and more neurotic by the hour.

Of course she would continue to interview other people—at least on Instant Messenger—until everything was worked out. But she was already pretty sure she'd found what she was looking for, the perfect mate.

Wait. Doesn't she mean *room*mate?!

b can't stop running away from home

"Excuse me. What are you guys doing?" Blair demanded. Eleanor Waldorf and Blair's stepbrother, Aaron Rose, were standing on the bed in Blair's makeshift bedroom, thumb-tacking some sort of large map to the wall. Blair stood in the doorway with her arms folded, awaiting an explanation.

"Don't tell," her mom whispered excitedly to Aaron. Eleanor was wearing a bizarre Versace outfit that had *bad sample-sale purchase* written all over it. The outfit consisted of an orange-and-black vertically striped halter top attached to green-and-black horizontally striped pedal-pushers by way of a mess of gold chains and buttons. The pedal-pushers even sported gold fringe.

Why is it that the mom population is always drawn to designers' biggest mistakes?

Not only was Eleanor's outfit ugly, but in another fit of postpartum depression she'd done something dreadful to her hair. That morning it had been shoulder-length and blond. Now it was dyed dark red and cropped close to her head, like Sharon Osbourne's. Needless to say, it was sort of hard for Blair to look at her.

Aaron pushed the last tack into the corner of the map and

hopped down from the bed, his wannabe Rastafarian mini dreadlocks banging merrily against his hollow vegan cheeks. "I hate to break it to you, Ma, but this is going to require just a wee bit of clarification." He shot Blair an apologetic look. "Sorry, sis, we wanted to surprise you."

Blair liked her stepbrother Aaron okay—much more than she liked his fat loser of a father, Cyrus Rose—but it totally infuriated her when he called Eleanor *Ma* or her *sis*. After all, his father and her mother had only been married since Thanksgiving, so Eleanor was very definitely not his mom and she was very definitely not his sister. Despite the existence of her little brother Tyler, who was a boy, and Yale, who was only a baby, Blair had always identified herself as an only child, except for those rare occasions when she and Serena were getting along so well it felt like they were sisters.

Eleanor scooted off the bed, grabbed Blair's hand, and dragged her over to the sage-colored wall to look at the map. It was a detail of Australia and the Pacific Ocean, and there were four red circles drawn around four pinpricks in the sea between Vanuatu and Fiji. Underneath the circles, written in black ink in Eleanor's loopy cursive, were the names *Yale*, *Tyler*, *Aaron*, and *Blair*.

Pardonnez-moi?

Blair twisted her ruby ring around and around on her finger. "What the fuck, Mom?" she demanded impatiently.

Eleanor was still holding Blair's hand and she squeezed her daughter's fingers tightly with manic delight. "I bought you an *island*, sweetie, and named it after you. Each of my four little darlings has their very own Pacific island! And next year, when they print the new maps, your names will appear right there next to Fiji! Isn't it fantastic?"

Blair stared at the map. Fiji had always sounded sort of

exotic to her, but the Island of Blair probably consisted of a scrappy shrub on top of a piece of reef riddled with spiny sea urchins and kelp.

"Tyler's already planning our big South Pacific Christmas trip next year," Eleanor rattled on. "He's researching which of our islands have the best surf."

"And your mom's buying each of us a board," Aaron informed her. "Except for Yale."

Blair noticed that Aaron's toenails were painted black.

"It's a band thing," he explained, noticing her noticing. "We were bonding over the fact that, at the moment, none of us has a girlfriend."

Big surprise, Blair thought. If he wasn't careful, Aaron was going to become one of those pale, skinny, asexual, vegetarian old men like Morrissey, fading into the ether without anyone remembering that he'd ever been there. Aaron and Serena had hooked up and even been in love for a fleeting moment that winter, but Aaron wasn't exciting enough to hold Serena's attention for more than five minutes.

Then again, who was?

Blair really wasn't all that interested in what Aaron and his loser Bronxdale Prep bandmates did to amuse themselves, or in her mother's insane need to buy random, completely pointless things like islands and alpacas and surfboards, but she did want to know what Kitty Minky, her Russian Blue cat, was doing digging around in the sumptuous pile of silk-covered bolsters, pillows, and throws at the head of her bed.

"Meow-meow?" Blair playfully addressed the cat in the made-up cat language she'd used with Kitty Minky since she was nine years old.

All of a sudden Kitty Minky let loose a stream of disgusting-smelling cat pee.

"No!" Blair shouted, hurling a putty-colored leather Manolo sandal at him. Kitty Minky leapt off the bed, but it was too late: Blair's rose-colored silk bedspread and throw pillows were soaked through.

"Oh my!" Eleanor exclaimed, wringing her hands and looking like she was about to cry. "Oh dear me, what a mess," she added despairingly, her mood shifting abruptly from high to low.

"Don't worry, Blair. You can sleep with me and Tyler in our room until Esther cleans this place up," Aaron offered.

Tyler and Aaron's room smelled like beer and feet and tofu hot dogs and those foul herbal cigarettes Aaron was always smoking. Blair wrinkled her nose. "I'd rather sleep on the floor in Yale's room," she responded miserably.

Eleanor wrung her hands. "Oh, but baby Yale's in quarantine for the next few days. She picked up some sort of terrible face rash at the pediatrician's office when she was there for her checkup yesterday. Apparently it's very contagious."

Ew.

Blair's small blue eyes narrowed. She adored her baby sister, but she wasn't about to risk getting a rash, especially not a *face* rash. Which left a particular question unanswered: Exactly where the fuck was she supposed to sleep?!

The penthouse was clearly uninhabitable, and while the Archibalds' house had seemed like an obvious choice only an hour ago, it had since turned into an after-school program for sixteen-year-old Nate-worshipping stoners. Serena's door was always open, but Serena's parents were kind of old-fashioned, and they probably wouldn't like it if Blair had a boy in her room with the door closed or whatever.

Like Serena never had a boy in her room with the door closed?!

Besides, Blair had already tried living with Serena for a few days that spring and they'd fought the whole time. Of course that was when Blair had been trying to seduce Serena's brother Erik in order to lure Nate away from that drugged-up lumber heiress he'd met in rehab. Still, now that she and Serena were friends again, it was best not to risk it.

As if they wouldn't find something *else* to fight over.

Blair pulled open the top drawer of the cruelty-free mahogany dresser. She had a credit card, and there were lots of nice hotels nearby. She grabbed a pair of clean white cotton Hanro underwear and a white tank top. The one benefit of wearing a uniform to school was packing light. And the benefit of packing light was that undoubtedly she would need something she didn't have and would therefore have to buy at one of the three *B*s: Bendel's, Bergdorf's, or Barneys.

"Want to come see what Tyler's found out about our islands?" Aaron offered. "He's downloading a whole bunch of stuff right now."

"The man I spoke to said the temperature on the islands is consistently between seventy-five and eighty-five degrees all year round," Eleanor added gleefully. She glanced at her gold Cartier chain-link wristwatch. "Phooey. I'm five minutes late for my Red Door makeup appointment." She giggled conspiratorially and clapped her hands together like a little girl. "Cyrus is taking me out to the Four Seasons tonight. I can't wait to surprise him with *his* present."

Blair didn't even want to guess what her mom could have dreamed up to buy Cyrus. A whole country?

"I'll probably be back to pick up a few things," she informed her mother. "And we definitely need a new mattress, pillows, and sheets for this room. But I'm not sure if I'll even be coming back, you know, to *live*."

Eleanor blinked dazedly at her daughter. After seventeen and a half years of being Blair's mother, she still didn't quite know what to make of her.

"Just in case there's a civil war on your island or your new shipment of French underwear comes in, exactly where might you be reached?" Aaron demanded with an annoying wise-assed smirk.

Blair smirked back. "The Plaza?"

And preferably a suite.

n is easily led out to sea

The roof terrace atop Nate's four-story town house wasn't high enough for a real view, but it was still nice to sit up there and suck hits out of Jeremy's giant green glass bong and reminisce about all the wild shit they'd gotten up to when they were young and carefree—before they had stuff to worry about like college and the future.

As if they were genuinely worried.

"Dude. Remember that time in Latin when you were so baked you thought you were in French?" Charlie Dern drawled, blowing smoke out of a tiny gap in the side of his wide, clownish mouth. "You were just babbling in French like a fucking lunatic and Mr. Herman the She-Man was like, 'I beg your pardon, Mr. Archibald. Although all romance languages find their roots in Latin, I never did master French.'"

Anthony Avuldsen and Jeremy Scott Tompkinson began to cackle as they remembered that legendary day.

"I was speaking fucking *perfect* French, too," Nate observed. "I think maybe for a moment there I thought I *was* French. Like a native speaker."

"Right," Charlie agreed sarcastically. "Man, you could barely even *talk*."

Lexie floated by in her tie-dyed dress, barefoot and waving her hands in front of her face. She'd drawn flowers on her fingers and toes with a glow-in-the-dark pen she'd found on Nate's desk, and they glowed neon green in the deepening twilight. A ponytailed boy named Malcolm was playing the guitar and singing an ancient James Taylor song.

You just call out my naaame
And you know where ever I aaam
I'll come runnin' to see you again.

"I wish we were at the beach." Jeremy sighed and traced his index finger along the rim of the bong. "Everything would be perfect if we were at the beach."

Nate nodded his golden brown head in agreement. "We will be soon. My parents' Hamptons booze cruise is in a couple weeks. Boat's already docked down in Battery Park. You're coming, right?"

The junior boys on the roof terrace looked up, wondering hopefully if Nate was addressing them.

Fat chance.

"*Everyone's* coming," Anthony Avuldsen responded, making the juniors feel like even worse dweebs. "It's like the kick-off to the whole freaking summer."

"Blair's class is doing their senior cut day the next day," Nate mused. He realized vaguely that Blair had never made an appearance on the roof terrace. Maybe she was still in the shower, or maybe she'd kissed him good-bye and gone home? He honestly couldn't remember. If she was in the shower, he might steal downstairs and surprise her. The thought of her wet and naked made him smile deliciously.

Charlie pulled a marijuana-stuffed Ziploc from out of his khaki pants pocket and began loading up the bong. "You said the boat's in the harbor?"

Before Nate had a chance to respond, his cell phone rang. BLAIR flashed up on the phone's little screen.

Speak of the she-devil.

Nate pressed answer and put the phone to his ear without actually saying anything.

"Guess where I am?" Blair gushed happily. "*The Plaza*. So get your ass over here right now. I have a suite."

The Plaza was only about twenty blocks away. Nate gazed in the general direction of downtown. It seemed very far away, but it would be nice to lie on a big white hotel bed and watch lots of movies and order room service. He was pretty hungry.

Not exactly what Blair had in mind.

"Just bring your toothbrush. I've got everything else covered," she added coyly.

Meaning the three Cs: champagne, caviar, and condoms.

"Sounds good," Nate responded gamely. "See you in a minute." He clicked off and Jeremy shoved the bong at him.

"So what I'm thinking is," he told Nate with the intense face of a seriously stoned person. He'd picked the green alligator away from his black Lacoste shirt, and it dangled from his chest like a partially removed scab. "We all head down to your parents' boat. It's stocked with booze, and the crew's probably doing the tourist thing in town and won't even notice if we take it out for a spin, right? You sail like a master. Why not go on a little pre-Hamptons excursion to, say—"

"Bermuda!" Charlie piped up.

"Fuck, yeah," Anthony agreed.

The three boys looked at Nate. They knew they were asking to do something completely outrageous, but they could tell by the interested glimmer in Nate's eye that he was sort of into it.

Nate's mind was racing in a blurry, zig-zaggedy, stoned way. Sail the boat to Bermuda? Sure, why not? They were seniors—they could do whatever they wanted. Blair could come too, and they could drink mimosas and make love on the beach under the warm sun. She was always talking about going away together.

Lexie came over and sat down in Nate's lap. She smelled like amber incense and goose-liver paté. The tip of her jet-black ponytail just grazed the sun, moon, and stars tattoo on her shoulder blade. "*Alors,* what's next?" she yawned, taking the bong from Nate.

Nate waited until she was done with the hit before pushing her out of his lap and hoisting himself to his feet. He clapped his hands together like a stoned camp counselor. "Come on, everybody, we're going on an adventure."

The junior boys began to murmur excitedly. Not only had they gotten to party at Nate Archibald's town house, he was *taking* them somewhere—probably somewhere cooler than they had ever been before.

"Anyone who pukes on boats should probably stay behind!" Jeremy warned.

"No fucking way," whispered a St. Jude's junior whose name happened to be Nate Lyons, and who mimicked his namesake down to the color of his navy blue Brooks Brothers socks. There was a mass rush for the exit. Nate Archibald, the coolest senior boy on the Upper East Side, was taking them out on his boat. It was their big fucking day!

Nate followed the rest of the boys downstairs with good-natured amusement, completely forgetting what he'd been about to do before the topic of a sail to Bermuda even came

up. Behind him, his cell phone lay forgotten on the roof terrace, its little screen flashing the name BLAIR as it rang every
two minutes for the next half hour.

Winter, spring, summer, or fa-waall
All you have to do is ca-waall
And I'll beee there!

Yeah. Right.

another wasted pair of la perla underwear

"Nate's on his way over," Blair announced to Serena smugly over the phone. She'd called Serena just to brag about being at the Plaza, feeling guilty as she dialed but getting over the guilt by the time the phone began to ring. She leaned toward the massive gilt-framed bathroom mirror and applied another coat of Chanel Vamp lipstick. It was dark red and she usually only wore it in winter, but when you were locked in a sumptuous hotel suite with your boyfriend having constant sex, who cared what season it was?

"Don't be mad," Blair pleaded with her best friend. "We can hang out in my suite tomorrow afternoon or something, okay?" She flashed her reflection a sexy, knowing grin. "*After* Nate and I wake up."

"You two are ridiculous," Serena scoffed without the slightest note of jealousy. Blair had confessed to finally losing her virginity to Nate the morning after it happened, but she'd resisted going into too much detail and Serena had resisted asking too many questions. After all, Serena and Nate had lost *their* virginities together, so sex with Nate was kind of an awkward subject.

"I have to go to this new Yale students' party," Serena

responded. "Not that I'm going to Yale," she hurriedly corrected herself. Her acceptance to Yale was an even worse subject. "My parents signed us up though, so I have to go."

"Oh." Blair pouted her lips and turned around to examine her butt in her new black silk La Perla underwear set. Of course she wasn't exactly into Yale *yet*, but she *was* on the fucking wait list—they still could have invited her.

"I was hoping you'd come with me," Serena added. "Since you're totally more likely to go to Yale than I am."

Blair readjusted her bra straps. Nate was into Yale too, but he hadn't mentioned any Yale party. And if he wasn't going, she certainly couldn't go. They might be . . . otherwise engaged.

Uh-huh.

"It's not until seven," Serena prompted. "You guys should be ready to venture outside by then."

"Can I call you about it tomorrow?" Blair asked dubiously.

"Whatever." Serena didn't mind going to parties by herself, since she was never by herself for very long. Boys buzzed and hovered around her like flies at a picnic. "Have fun tonight. 'Bye, sweetie."

Blair hung up just as the bellboy arrived with the bottle of Dom Pérignon and the plate of caviar and toast points she'd ordered from room service. She slipped into one of the Plaza's thick white terrycloth robes and answered the door.

"Over by the bed," she commanded, loving how Joan Crawfordishly jaded she sounded. She tipped the guy and waited until he'd closed the door. Then she slipped out of her robe, flopped down on her side on the massive California king bed, and reached for the remote. Within seconds she'd found AMC—American Movie Classics, the channel that regularly played all her favorites like *Breakfast at Tiffany's*, starring Audrey Hepburn, and *My Fair Lady*, also starring Audrey Hepburn.

To her disappointment, *Dirty Dancing* was playing. Since when was anything made after 1980 a true *classic*? Blair wondered. All of a sudden she felt old. But then, that seemed sort of appropriate, considering the fact that she was about to have a hot-and-heavy liaison with her lover in a sumptuous hotel suite. Where was Nate anyway? A cab from his house to the Plaza would only take about seven minutes. If she were Nate, she'd have made it in five. She dialed his cell without even looking at the buttons on her phone, but there was no answer. Maybe he was showering and putting on his sexy black Calvin Klein boxers in preparation for their rendezvous, she mused.

Or maybe not.

Blair stood up, removed her robe, and dimmed the lights. Then she spread a little caviar on one of the toast points and stood watching herself in the oversized gilt-framed dressing mirror as she ate it. On the TV screen behind her, "Baby" was trying to look innocent after spending all night having big sweaty sex with Patrick Swayze, the dance instructor at the summer resort where her family was vacationing. Baby's dad was so seriously pissed off at her, Blair wondered fleetingly how her own dad would feel if he knew she'd moved into a hotel suite just so she could have a little privacy with Nate. Not that her gay, French-château-living, pastel-argyle-socks-and-baby-blue-Gucci-sunglasses-wearing dad and Baby's responsible doctor dad in *Dirty Dancing* had anything in common. She dialed Nate once again and when he didn't answer, she made herself another caviar toast point sandwich and called her dad's number in southern France, where he'd been living since he and Eleanor split up over his gayness almost two years ago.

"Bear? Is everything okay? Did you hear from those fuck-heads at Yale yet? Are you in?" her father demanded as soon as he heard her voice.

Blair could picture him perfectly, naked except for a pair of royal blue silk boxer shorts, his sleeping lover—François or Eduard or whatever his name was—snoring softly beside him. Harold Waldorf, Esq. used to be managing partner at a major corporate law firm, married to society hostess Eleanor and living in a penthouse with his two lovely children, Blair and Tyler. Now he bottled his own wine from the vineyards surrounding his château, shopped at cute French boutiques that catered exclusively to tanned gay men, and swam laps in his pool while his tanned gay lovers attended him with fresh towels and glasses of cognac.

It was a luxe life, indeed.

"Guess where I am?" Blair boasted in the same tone she'd used to talk to Serena. In fact, talking to her dad was exactly like talking to one of her girlfriends. He didn't even mind that it was almost two in the morning in France and she had totally woken him up.

"Paris?" her dad asked hopefully. "I'll send a car for you. You'll be here in an hour."

"No, Dad," Blair whined, although she honestly wouldn't have minded being in Paris—as long as she could bring Nate and her suite at the Plaza with her. "I'm at the Plaza. I'm living here now. In a suite."

"You go, girl!" her dad exclaimed. "I guess the penthouse might be a little crowded with the new baby and all."

In the background Blair heard the sound of him pouring something into a glass. He was so into his latest batch of white wine, he probably kept a bottle chilling next to the bed exactly for occasions like this.

In *Dirty Dancing* Land, Baby's bitchy sister was performing in a stupid talent show, wearing a bikini top that was way too small for her. Blair muted the TV, spread another blob of caviar on a toast point, lit a cigarette, and sighed dramatically. "It's just that I'm almost graduating and I need space—you know, to do my work and think about next year and . . ."

All of a sudden she had a very clear image of herself as a sort of reclusive Greta Garbo–like movie star who rarely left her hotel room, communicating with the outside world only through the roles she decided to play. The staff would pick through her trash and steal her clothes, and tourists would stand on Central Park South opposite the hotel, just waiting to catch a glimpse of her. She'd be the talk of the town.

As if she wasn't already.

"Oh, I'll bet you're *working*," her dad scoffed between sips of whatever it was he was drinking. "I bet that hunky boyfriend of yours is massaging your feet as we speak."

If only.

Blair giggled and scarfed down another caviar sandwich between drags on her Merit Ultra Light. "Actually, Nate's on his way over," she admitted. She contemplated the bottle of champagne she'd ordered, still chilling in its silver-plated ice bucket. Nate wouldn't mind if she opened the bottle and had one tiny glass before he arrived, would he?

Of course not.

"I thought as much," her dad replied knowingly. "But you deserve it, sweetie. You deserve to have it all."

As if she didn't already know that.

Blair grabbed the bottle of champagne and held it between her bare knees, expertly untwisting the wire keeper from around the cork and then inching the cork out of the bottle's neck, slowly . . . slowly . . . until . . .

Pop!

"Oh. My. God. You are so totally having a party!" her father exclaimed. "On a *school night*?" he added, pretending to be horrified, as if he were a strict parent who actually cared about things like that. "Let me talk to that hunky boyfriend of yours *right now*."

Blair filled a champagne flute, guzzled the entire contents, and then refilled it. On-screen Patrick Swayze was face-to-face with Baby's dad. "Nobody puts Baby in a corner," Blair mouthed the words, even though the TV had been muted. It was the cheesiest movie, but she still fantasized about Nate defending her in such a determined, angry way. Nate was seriously hot when he was angry, which was just about . . . never.

It's hard to get riled up when you're stoned all the time.

"I told you, Dad," Blair corrected, "Nate's not here yet." She gritted her teeth and took another gulp of champagne. Although who knew what was taking him so goddamned long. "Anyway"—she pouted her lips for the mirror or the camera or whoever happened to be spying on her through a telescope from the treetops in Central Park—"if I deserve to have it all, then how come stupid Yale hasn't let me in yet?"

"Oh, Bear," her dad sighed in his manly-but-motherly voice that made both men *and* women fall in love with him instantly. "They will, dammit. They *will* let you in."

Blair reached for another toast point and discovered she'd eaten them all. Over the phone she heard someone mumble something in sleepy French.

"Look, Sugar Bear, it's late. I have to go." Her dad spoke

over the mumbling. "You're okay though, right? You just enjoy yourself."

Blair looked askance at the half-empty bottle of champagne and the crumbs of caviar scattered on the white china plate. *Dirty Dancing* had ended. "Good night, Dad," she replied, feeling a little sad. She hung up and dialed Nate's cell phone again. No answer. She dialed his house line. No answer, just his uptight admiral dad on the answering machine, reading from the actual instructions the machine came with that no normal person ever used: "You have reached the Archibald residence. Please leave a brief message and we will return your call as soon as possible."

A Streetcar Named Desire, starring Marlon Brando and Vivien Leigh, was just about to start. Another old favorite. Blair put the white terrycloth bathrobe back on and fluffed up the pillows on the giant bed. Then she dialed room service again. "A hot fudge sundae, please. And a pack of Merit Ultra Lights."

She sank back on the pillows and closed her eyes. When she'd left his house, Nate had been partying with a bunch of stoners, including an annoying French hippie chick named Lexique. That stupid, lazy *asshole* who so didn't deserve to go to Yale probably hadn't even noticed that Blair had left. Tears seeped out from under her closed lids. Nate hadn't changed. Nothing had changed—except the status of her virginity. She bit her lip and fought back an angry sob. *Well, so what?* Nate didn't deserve sex. Besides, eating a hot fudge sundae in a Plaza Hotel bed while plotting her revenge on her asshole-of-a-loser-soon-to-be-ex-boyfriend was even better than sex.

Way better.

k and *i* take their jobs super-seriously

Dear Seniors,

We are so excited for next Friday, which as you know is Senior Cut Day, now known as the first day of SENIOR SPA WEEKEND!!!!! Yes, it's a school day. Unfortunately we'll be too busy getting ready for our hot-stone facials and seaweed body wraps to remember to show up! Please don't be worried about getting into trouble—not that you really are. Senior Cut Day is an ancient Constance Billard School tradition, and no one's ever been expelled or even punished for it.

So here's what's happening:

Thursday night at 6:30 P.M. we'll board the Archibald family's big sailboat, which is docked at Battery Park City. The Archibalds are having their annual benefit cruise to the Hamptons, and they've generously offered us a ride. As soon as we dock in Sag Harbor, we'll be picked up by a fleet of limos, which will whisk us off to Isabel Coates's totally amazing beach house, where the biggest, bestest girls-only slumber party will take place. NO BOYS ALLOWED. In the morning we'll have breakfast by the pool, catered by . . .TBA (we're working on getting the chef who helped Julia Roberts lose all that weight after having her twins). After that, a day of treatments brought to us by Origins. And everyone will get an Origins gift bag valued at three hundred dollars to take home with her totally refreshed and revitalized new self!

Dress: Resort casual. Towels, hairdryers, bath, and beauty products galore will all be supplied. No dogs, please, even if they're really small. And NO BOYS!

Let's hear it for an amazing weekend of bonding with the girls!

Big Smoochies!!

> Love,
>
> Your classmates Kati Farkas and Isabel Coates

P.S. We put a suggestion box in the senior lounge, so your ideas are welcome, not that we haven't already planned the most perfect day!

P.P.S. Two, four, six, eight, only one month till we graduate!!!

Disclaimer: All the real names of places, people, and events have been altered or abbreviated to protect the innocent. Namely, me.

hey people!

Some recent observations

The castaways

I honestly don't know what's gotten into a certain group of people lately. I mean is it okay to just, like, disappear?? Apparently a bunch of boys we all know and love (at least *most* of the time) have hijacked a very large, well-appointed sailboat and are headed into the Atlantic. It could be just another senior prank, except that half the boys on the boat are juniors. It's kind of a random time to take off, especially when all of us girls could use a little entertainment. Just who do they think they are—Christopher Columbus?

You heard it here first

They have their choice of guys, but for whatever reason, models can't get enough of guys with guitars. Rumor has it the latest couple of the moment is a certain blond-haired Fifth Avenue–dwelling senior girl and the lead guitarist from the Raves. How, when, and where they met is a complete mystery, but talk about a perfect couple!

To Gap or not to Gap?

Don't even try to pretend it was someone else: I saw you sneaking into the Gap on Eighty-sixth and Madison and actually trying on a plum-colored imitation Juicy Couture terrycloth zip-up hoodie in the kids' section. Okay, I'm a snooping bitch. But the reason I'm ratting you out is I tried the very same hoodie on, and, unlike you (although I know you wanted to), I bought three of them! Why not? They're *cute*, and we're going to need lots of terrycloth cover-ups to wear après le pool this summer. Plus we'll probably spill Campari or crème de menthe or something equally devastating all over ourselves, so we'll need more than one. Besides, terrycloth is terrycloth, and what better way to show off your new white jacquard Gucci bikini than with a cute plum-colored hoodie? Think of this as a get-out-of-jail-free card: you're still not allowed to buy your jeans there—heaven forbid—but you now have my permission to purchase certain necessary items at the Gap.

Your e-mail

Q: Dear GG,
Are you ever going to tell us where you're going to college next year? Have you even decided?
—qrs

A: Dear qrs,
That's for me to know and you to find out. But let me ask you this—do I strike you as the indecisive type?
—GG

Q: Dear GG,
I heard Damian Polk from the Raves used to live in the same building as that blond model you're always talking about. They've known each other since they were babies and they used to hook up in the elevator in the middle of the night, while the doorman was napping.
—ob-v-us

A: Dear ob-v-us,
That's a great story, but I heard Damian's family lived in Ireland until he was like thirteen. Hence his funny accent and the reason why he always seems a little drunk.
—GG

Q: Dear GG,
I run the crew on a sailboat that belongs to a prominent New York family. The son, who I hear has been in lots of trouble before, took off in the sailboat yesterday evening and hasn't

returned. I'm afraid his ass will be grass whenever he gets back, because his dad is kind of tough.
—captain

Dear captain,
His ass is already grass, for more reasons that that!
—GG

Sightings

S and an unidentified blond hunk—possibly her brother or possibly that guitarist from **the Raves**—at the **Central Park Zoo**, feeding left-over sushi from lunch at **Nicole's** to the sea lions. **B** buying two **La Perla** nighties at **Barneys**. She seems to have developed an addic-tion to lingerie, but what else can one wear while lounging alone in a **Plaza Hotel** suite, waiting for one's boyfriend to turn up? **D** at **Yellow Rat Bastard** on lower Broadway, trying on every hat in the store. **V** purchasing a new lip ring—ew!—at a piercing place in **Williamsburg**. **J** in **Barneys Co-op** trying on every pair of **Seven Jeans** in the store and ignoring the salesperson's suggestion that she'd have better luck finding jeans that fit in **Bloomingdale's** children's department. **K** and **I** at **Jackson Hole** again, scheming again. **N**—not. Where the hell is **N** anyway?

Don't worry, I'll find him.

You know you love me,

gossip girl

models who date rock stars

"How come no matter what I wear I always look like a cartoon character?" Jenny complained to her friend and Constance Billard School classmate Elise Wells. It was Saturday night and they were getting ready for Dan's gig with the Raves at Funktion, a new music venue in a revamped fire station on Orchard Street. Jenny glanced at Elise. "And you always look so normal."

The two girls regarded their reflections in the full-length mirror on the back of Jenny's closet door. Jenny was wearing a stretchy red top with cap sleeves and a plunging U-shaped neckline that made her breasts look gargantuan. She was barely five feet tall, and her very first pair of Seven jeans had been way too long for her when she bought them at Bloomingdale's, so she'd had the lady at the dry cleaner's on Broadway and Ninety-eighth shorten them about ten inches. Now she noticed that the purposely "antiqued" spot on each leg where her knees were supposed to be fell at mid-shin. The only acceptable part of Jenny's body was her head. She liked her big, far-apart brown eyes, her clear white skin, her red lips, and her curly brown hair with its straight, severe bangs across the forehead. As Serena once told her, she looked like a Prada model—with oversized breast implants and stumps for legs, although Serena would never have said that part.

Elise's body was totally the opposite. She was seven inches taller than Jenny, with long skinny legs, long skinny arms, and a flat chest. Nothing was ever too tight on her, except maybe in the belly region, which had a sort of doughnut roll around it. But that was easily hidden beneath a shirt. There was really nothing Jenny could do to hide her chest. Then again, Elise was covered with freckles—there were even freckles on her eyelids—and she had chin-length straw-yellow hair that was so thick and so coarse, she could barely fit it into a rubber band.

Well, nobody's perfect. Except for maybe a very select few of us.

"Let's trade tops," Elise suggested. She pulled off her black V-neck T-shirt and handed it to Jenny.

"Okay," Jenny responded dubiously, and pulled off her red one. Elise's shirt was from Express, and hers was from Anthropologie, which was slightly nicer, but Jenny didn't want to hurt Elise's feelings by saying anything. Besides, the results were astronomical. Jenny's chest looked almost modest in the black top, and the red top made Elise's hair gleam with strawberry highlights neither of them had even known she had.

"I bet Serena van der Woodsen doesn't even look at herself before she goes out," Jenny declared. She dropped down on her knees and started crawling around the room. "She probably doesn't even have to try stuff on, except for maybe shoes."

Elise put her hands on her hips. "What are you doing?"

"Wearing in the knees on my jeans," Jenny replied, still crawling. "Did you hear about Serena and Damian from the Raves?"

Jenny stood on tiptoe and then eased her heels back into her shoes again. "Lucky we're on the guest list," she sighed, "or they'd never let us in."

Actually, with a chest like that she could probably get in anywhere. But let her find that out for herself.

v can be such a girl sometimes

"What the fuck?" Vanessa demanded. How she had missed them after all these years she had no idea. She twisted her head around and checked her reflection in the bathroom mirror once again. There they were, four big brown moles, all lined up on her neck behind her ear like some kind of fucked-up constellation. She felt like a girl in a Clearasil commercial, panicking because she'd gotten a zit right before going out on a date. Zits were temporary, though. The moles were there to stay. Who in her right mind would keep her head shaved with moles like that on her neck?

She yanked open a drawer beneath the bathroom sink, looking for some of that skin-colored cover-up crap her sister Ruby put under her eyes when she'd been up all night. She found a stick of something called Peekaboo that was a little pinker than her natural skin tone but good enough. She dabbed some over the moles, rubbed it in, and examined the results. Now she looked like she had poison ivy, or poison neck. She considered pasting a Band-Aid across the whole area, but she didn't have one big enough to cover all four of the moles, and a Band-Aid would only draw attention to the problem. She washed off the cover-up and then dug around in the drawer, looking for something that might distract Beverly from the hideous deformities on her neck.

As if the still-healing lip piercing on her upper lip wasn't distracting enough. Beverly had been polite enough not to mention it before, but now that they were getting to know each other, he might ask if the crusty sore beneath that silver D-ring actually hurt.

And why would Beverly even want to check out her neck? They were only going to the Raves gig together—just hanging out to see if they'd mind cohabitating, as in *roommates,* not lovers who looked at each other's necks. Besides, Beverly was an artist. He might think her moles were cool.

A sample vial of perfume called Certainty was rolling around in the bottom of the messy vanity drawer. It sounded like the name of a tampon or a pregnancy test, but Vanessa eased the little black cap off the vial and dabbed some perfume on her wrists and temples anyway. Certainty smelled musky and powerful and might be so distracting to Beverly that he wouldn't even notice her disgusting configuration of neck moles. Maybe it would even work some sort of magic. She would walk into the club where Dan and the Raves were playing; Dan would turn purple with a mixture of desire, regret, and mad jealousy; and Beverly would feel immediately certain about wanting to live with her. As a friend, of course.

Of course.

it sucks when your mood and your outfit don't match

"Sure you're all right, man?" Damian asked for the second time through the locked bathroom stall door.

"Yep," Dan called back from the other side of the door, praying that Damian and the rest of the band would think this was just his usual pre-gig behavior and go back to playing poker and knocking back Stoli shots or whatever they were doing backstage.

"All right, then. See you in a few," Damian replied. "Nice shoelaces," he added before leaving the bathroom.

Perched on top of the toilet seat lid, Dan stared woefully down at his new sneakers and the absurdly wide pant legs that nearly covered them. Yesterday he'd wandered into 555 Soul on Broadway in SoHo and let a sales guy talk him into a completely new performance wardrobe. Big yellow-and-black two-tone T-shirt, insanely huge and baggy gray rip-stop pants with drawstrings and toggles and pockets all over them, black canvas Converse sneakers with yellow laces, and a khaki-colored truckers' hat with a picture of a yellow YIELD sign on it. The hat kept his wild, shaggy hair under control and revealed his shaved neck, making him look more menacing than he'd ever thought possible. In fact, with his new outfit, he kind of looked like a shorter, skinnier Eminem. Which was really not the look he wanted at all.

None of the guys in the band had commented on his outfit when he showed up, but then again he hadn't really given them time. One look at the huge line forming outside the club and the instruments and microphones set up on the stage inside had sent him rushing to the bathroom to puke his guts out. He'd been locked in a stall ever since.

If only he had a lucky talisman like a handmade silver belt buckle or a shark tooth necklace the way most legendary rock singers probably did. He could don his lucky whatever-it-was, his nervousness would disappear, and he'd perform with complete abandon, driving the crowd insane. Instead, he just sat on the toilet in the club's garish pea-green-painted men's room and smoked his lucky Camels—about forty of them— feeling progressively sicker and sicker.

All of a sudden the men's room door creaked open and the scuffed toes of Damian's black work boots appeared under the stall door once more. "Have a taste and you'll be all right," he advised, shoving an unopened bottle of Stoli under the door.

Dan took the bottle. If he was going to perform tonight he'd need to feel as fly as his outfit. He opened it and took a swig. His stomach felt so bottomless and endless, it was like pouring a teaspoon of vodka into an empty well. He took another swig and wiped his mouth on the back of his hand.

"See you in a few then, yeah?" Damian said again. "You might want to lose the hat, though," he added gently before leaving the men's room.

The Raves were all about not having a look and not trying too hard. Most of them still wore the clothes their moms had bought them in prep school—Lacoste polo shirts, Brooks

Brothers khakis—paired with something cool and absurdly expensive, like a custom-made kidskin trench coat from Dolce & Gabbana. But Dan's mom had fled to the Czech Republic with some balding, horny count before he'd even started high school, so he didn't even own any polo shirts or khakis, only the clothes he picked out for himself and paid for with the barely adequate clothing allowance Rufus gave him. He could feel his panic mounting. Who was going to want to listen to a sick, skinny high-school kid with a shaved neck wearing fashion-disaster yellow-and-black shoes?

You'd be surprised.

you're beautiful and your mother dresses you funny

Skirt, shirt, bra, underwear, shoes, watch, pearl choker, pearl earrings—Serena stared at the clothes her mom had laid out neatly on the end of her canopy bed. Everything her mom had chosen was gray or navy blue, which just happened to be Yale University's colors.

Hello, dorkdom! Did she really need her mom to pick out her clothes? How old was she, anyway—five?

Her parents were in their suite of rooms, getting ready for Yale University's Yale Loves New York party for incoming freshmen from New York City at Stanford Parris III's apartment on Park Avenue and Eighty-fourth Street. For them it was just another cocktail party—a chance to mingle with the parents of the children their own children had gone to school and tennis lessons and SAT prep with for most of their lives. No one would know each other intimately, but everyone would know everyone. People like the van der Woodsens thought of everyone in their circle as their dearest friends, but how intimate did you really want to be with someone like Stanford Parris III?

"Are you almost ready, dear?" Serena heard her mother call out to her.

"Yeah," she called back, feeling stubborn and grumpy and

annoyed. After all, she could have been on her way to the Raves gig right now instead of to another totally boring and useless party with her *parents*. Ignoring the outfit her mother had selected for her, she sat down in front of her iMac and logged on. Most of the e-mails were from fashion houses like Burberry and Missoni, announcing sample sales or parties to launch a signature fragrance or shoe, but a new message from someone at Brown topped the list, followed by a message from Harvard, and one from Princeton.

To: SvW@vanderWoodsen.com
From: apainter@brown.edu

Carina Serena,
I used to paint faceless angels and hands
without bodies. I used to be dead. Now my
art has a face, and to have you here at
Brown next year—oh living, breathing
muse!—would be my resurrection.
I kneel at your feet.
Christian
P.S. There is a rumor you are engaged to
that madman lead guitarist in the Raves.
My love, I pray this is only a rumor.

To: SvW@vanderWoodsen.com
From: bboy@harvarduniversity.edu

Dear Serena,
I know you and I are cut from a different
cloth, so to speak—I'm a jock from the
boondocks and you're a goddess from New

York City—but to quote a line from an old
song, I just can't get you out of my head.
When I think about you, the windows in my
Jeep steam up and I can't breathe. I'm
going to fail my finals because of you. I
don't think they make you repeat grades if
you fail a term in college the way they do
in high school, but I wouldn't mind if
they did, because then we'd be together
for even longer. I know this is kind of
crazy to say, but you're my girl, so you
better come to Harvard next year. Here's
to us for the next four years and forever.
Love,
Wade (your Harvard tour guide's roommate—
remember me?)

To: SvW@vanderWoodsen.com
From: Sheri@PrincetonTriDs.org

Dear Serena,
Just wanted you to know that we can NOT
stop talking about how you and Damian from
the Raves are like THE perfect couple!! We
are TOO excited to meet him, but first we
have to take down all the pictures of him
plastered all over our house—SO embarrassing! Give Damian a kiss for us, and tell
him we love him too (even though we'd
NEVER try to steal away your guy).
Love,
Your sisters, the Princeton Tri Delts

Serena winced and deleted all three stalkerish messages from her computer, hoping to delete the last one from her brain. There was nothing worse than a bunch of girls pretending to be your best friends when you didn't even know them, all gossiping about you and your new rock star boyfriend whom you'd never even met. Way to make her not want to go to college at all!

She logged off without reading the rest of her mail and pulled her luxurious fair hair back into a messy ponytail with a plain white rubber band. Then she smeared her lips with Vaseline and opened her bedroom door to look for her parents.

The elder van der Woodsens had their own suite of rooms consisting of a large bedroom with a massive four-poster bed, two dressing rooms with huge walk-in closets, two full bathrooms, and a lounge with a wet bar they never used, a plasma TV they never watched, and a library full of rare books they never read, because they were always out at charity dinners or the opera or watching polo matches up in Connecticut. It could have been an apartment all by itself, but it took up only a quarter of the van der Woodsens' entire Fifth Avenue spread.

"Didn't you see the clothes I laid out for you?" her mother demanded, sweeping her dark blue eyes despairingly over her daughter. Mrs. van der Woodsen was tall and fair like Serena, with the same symmetrical features, which had grown haughtily handsome with age. "Jeans with holes in the behind really aren't acceptable for this sort of occasion, don't you agree, dear?"

"They're not just any old jeans," Serena said, looking down at her faded pants. "They're my favorites."

Actually, she owned around twenty pairs of jeans, but

this particular pair of Blue Cults were this week's can't-live-without-them.

"The skirt and blouse I chose for you are just right," her mother insisted. She buttoned the jacket of her gold Chanel suit and glanced at the antique platinum Cartier wristwatch fastened to her slim, Santo Domingo–tanned wrist. "We're leaving in five minutes. Your father and I will be reading the newspapers in his study. Don't be difficult, darling. It's just a party. You like parties."

"Not this kind of party," Serena grumbled. Her mother raised her thin gray-blond eyebrows so fiercely she decided not to mention that she'd much rather see the Raves play than schmooze with a bunch of kids and their parents all gloating about the fact that they'd gotten into one of the toughest colleges to get into in the world.

Serena went back to her room and grudgingly changed out of her jeans and into the gray pleated Marc Jacobs skirt laid out on her bed, pairing it with a beaded aqua-colored T-shirt and her orange Miu Miu clogs instead of the boring navy blue blouse and baby blue suede Tod's loafers her mother had chosen.

And the pearls? Sorry, Mom.

Her last effort was to pull out the messy ponytail and run her fingers through her pale blond hair. Then, without even a glance in the mirror, she strode out of her room and into the front hall.

If only we could all be so sure of our exquisite beauty.

"Mom! Dad! I'm ready!" she trilled, trying to sound excited about it. She'd give the party five or ten minutes—just enough time for her parents to get involved in some supremely boring and involved conversation with Stanford Parris III or one of the other ancient dull Yale alumni who'd

been attending these parties for centuries, then she'd slip out
and head downtown to the Raves gig.

After all, if she was going to spend the next four years
being intellectual, she needed to enjoy herself while she had
the chance.

As if she didn't always enjoy herself.

drifting, drifting, over the ocean blue!

Jeremy, Charlie, and Anthony would not shut up about Bermuda, so when they got onboard the *Charlotte,* named after Nate's deceased paternal grandmother, Nate did a search for ports in Bermuda on the boat's computer and then programmed Horseshoe Bay into the navigational system. He set the motor for .5 miles per hour. That meant they were headed to Bermuda *very slowly*. In fact, even though they'd left the dock in lower Manhattan nearly twenty hours ago, they were only just drifting past Coney Island, in Brooklyn.

Friday night had oozed into Saturday night, and the sun hung low over Staten Island as the sailboat motored slowly southward. The air was cooler than on land and smelled like wet dog. Nate and everyone else on the boat remained stoned, sprawled on deck with their eyes half closed and their mouths hanging lazily open, or drifting languidly belowdecks in bare feet to replenish their stashes of beer and snacks.

It had dawned on Nate only recently that Blair wasn't onboard. He recalled that she'd called him last night from the Plaza, and that he'd sort of blown off meeting her. Of course he would have called her, but his cell phone was missing, and when he tried using Jeremy's phone, he discovered that he'd only ever speed-dialed Blair from his stored address book, and he didn't even know her number. And when you've been stoned for almost twenty-four hours, doing something like calling information to find your girlfriend's number seems impossibly complicated.

Hello, lameness?

Nate and his father had built the *Charlotte* themselves, up on the Archibald compound on Mt. Desert Island, Maine. It was a one-hundred-and-ten-foot ketch, huge enough to comfortably ferry one hundred–plus passengers from Battery Park City to the Hamptons, or seventeen high-school kids to Bermuda. In preparation for the upcoming cruise to the Hamptons, the kitchen had been fully stocked with artisanal cheeses, Carr's table water crackers, smoked oysters, Belgian beer, Veuve Clicquot champagne, and vintage scotch. The four bathrooms were equipped with hot showers, navy blue Frette towels, and handmade shell-shaped mini soaps with CHARLOTTE printed on them in gold. The cabin was equipped with the latest computer mapping and communication systems, and there were state-of-the-art sound systems both on deck and belowdecks.

After a dinner of beer, Brie, and potato chips, Nate passed up another session of bong hits with his buddies and climbed up into the crow's nest at the top of the taller of the boat's two masts. He sat down and hugged his knees, contemplating the situation from up high. Since they were only drifting, he was pretty sure they weren't going to get farther than the New Jersey shore before Monday, which was fine with him. He was also pretty sure he was just about to miss that Yale party he was supposed to go to with his parents. And he'd probably missed a whole slew of Blair's pissed-off, upset, and maybe even worried calls.

Probably.

Nate had the nagging feeling that this little foray onboard the *Charlotte* had been kind of a mistake. The crew would be frantic to find the boat missing, and his dad would be pissed as hell. But as long as they were back by the time the Hamptons cruise was supposed to start, there was no harm done, right? He lifted up his worn black T-shirt and checked to see if the hickey Blair had left on his belly the day before was still there. A shade lighter, but yes, still there. Just thinking about Blair eased his mind. Even if she was pissed off at him eighty percent of the time, they would stay together for always, and hopefully even go to Yale together. How good it was, he thought, as only a par-baked boy can, knowing you had someone's hand to hold when you were about to step into the big bad unknown.

"Peace, dude!" a girl's voice called up to him from the deck. "*Alors,* I found some Oreos for our dessert!"

Nate peered down at Lexie. From where he sat she looked very small and bright-eyed, like a little girl. All over the deck, groups of guys and a few girls were smoking and drinking blond Belgian beer out of crystal beer steins. In the aft of the boat the lazy music of one of Nate's mom's French jazz CDs wafted out of Bose waterproof speakers.

"Want one?" Lexie added. "I can climb up."

For a moment, Nate didn't respond. He shifted his gaze to the brightly lit Coney Island Ferris wheel, turning slowly round and round across the twinkling, greenish-brown water. He was pretty sure he didn't want Lexie to join him in the crow's nest. First of all, there was hardly room up there for one person; second of all, if she did, the obvious thing would be for him to kiss her, because she was pretty and had that sexy tattoo, and because she so obviously had a crush on him.

But these days he really didn't feel like kissing anyone but Blair. After all, he and Blair were supposed to be going to college together and getting married. They were going to spend their whole lives together.

Wait. Is he, like, having some sort of *epiphany*?

Nate stood up and began to climb down out of the crow's nest. He couldn't sit up there all night, waiting for the boat to turn itself around. Not when Blair was waiting for him, not when he had his whole future ahead of him.

He jumped down from the ladder and Lexie handed him an Oreo. "The water makes me feel so free," she declared, swaying slightly as the *Charlotte* drifted over a patch of rough water. Her tie-dyed dress had somehow loosened or gotten torn, and the cap sleeves drooped down over the tops of her arms, revealing her tanned shoulders and making the most of her tiny sun, moon, and stars tattoo.

Nate took an Oreo, pulled the two halves apart, and licked the white icing inside. Yes, he had his whole future ahead of him, but sometimes it's important to enjoy the simple things in life.

the isle of B

"Will you be dining here tonight, or shall we have your food sent down to your rooms at the Plaza, miss?" Aaron asked in his best hoity-toity English butler voice.

Blair glared at the annoying dreadlocked head that had poked its way into her so-called bedroom. "Actually, I'm going out," she replied, yanking a never-worn Calvin Klein navy blue satin slip dress out of her closet. Nate was still MIA and she'd just had the humiliating experience of taking a cab home from the Plaza in her school uniform, even though it was Saturday and there was no school.

Girls who must wear uniforms to school try their hardest not to be seen in uniform outside of school hours, and *especially* not on weekends.

Earlier that afternoon she'd actually had a pair of Earl jeans delivered to her room at the Plaza directly from Barneys Co-op, but when the jeans arrived they were a totally different style than the ones she was used to wearing—pencil straight and meant to ride so low that at least six inches of butt crack would show. Blair could barely get them over her knees. And, with only her school uniform, her La Perla underwear, and a white terrycloth Plaza Hotel bathrobe to wear, and nothing to do but watch TV for sixteen hours straight, she'd slowly been going insane. The Yale party Serena had mentioned would offer a welcome escape, as well as provide an opportunity to take revenge on Nate.

Roll camera.

She'd arrive at the party in a cloud of perfume and cigarette smoke, like some sort of genie, wearing something so adorably irresistible that all the incoming freshman boys and even the stodgy old Yale alumnae at the party would toss back their scotches and fall on their knees at her immaculately manicured feet. She'd have a torrid, newsworthy affair with the handsomest, most influential one in the bunch, making sure Nate heard all about it, and then demand that the aforementioned alumnus secure her acceptance at Yale. *Then* she'd tell Nate to go fuck himself and go to Brown or someplace even farther away, because she honestly never wanted to see his sorry face again.

"Nate's mom called. She was kind of snippy. Said she'd appreciate it if you and Nate showed up at the Yale Loves New York party tonight," Aaron informed her.

Huh?

Blair frowned down at the slip dress in her hands. It was a lovely shade of deep Yale blue, but not quite as come-hither as she would have liked. Unless she wore an outrageously sexy pair of strappy high-heeled sandals with it—of which she had many.

"I thought that party was only for people who were definitely *going* to Yale in the fall," Aaron persisted nosily. "You didn't get in already, did you?"

Ignoring him, Blair pulled one of those mini poncho things she didn't even remember buying from out of her closet. It was a sort of stripy blue-gray, one of Missoni's latest weaves. She held it against the dress to see if it would go, and it did, but it wasn't exactly the alluring you-know-you-want-me look she needed to set those Yalie hearts aflutter.

She threw Aaron an icy get-the-fuck-out-of-here-I'm-trying-to-get-dressed glance. "For your information, no, I didn't find out—*yet*. However, I am confident that eventually I *will* get in, so I really don't see why I shouldn't attend this party." She walked over to the door and gripped the doorknob, preparing to slam it in Aaron's face. He'd gotten into Harvard early admission. What the fuck did he care?

Aaron backed away, holding up his hands to show that he meant no harm. "No need to be so hostile."

Nothing makes a girl feel more hostile than being accused of being hostile.

Blair slammed the door. A few minutes later, she opened it again, wearing the royal blue slip dress and a pair of silver metallic three-and-a-half-inch Manolo sandals. She teetered down the hall to her old room. Baby Yale had the perfect notice-me accessory for her outfit. If Blair could just sneak into the nursery without anyone seeing. . .

Yale's room was decorated in shades of pale yellow and peach and was filled with plush toys and miniature wooden furniture. The crib was draped with thick white mosquito netting imported from India, so that it was impossible to see if Yale was sleeping inside it or not, but there was a hush about the room that suggested she was. It also suggested that the baby was still in quarantine.

Oops.

Blair tiptoed up to the buttery yellow antique armoire, slid open the top drawer, and removed a small white velvet jewelry box. Then she closed the door and tiptoed over to the crib.

"I'll bring it back, I promise," she whispered to the blanketed bundle lying peacefully inside. She lifted up the mosquito netting and planted a kiss on Yale's soft pink cheek, too focused on her prize to notice that the baby was wearing little mittens on her hands to keep her from scratching her rosy, rash-ridden body.

Usually it's the younger sister who steals stuff from her older sister's room, but, as baby Yale will eventually find out, Blair isn't exactly your average older sister.

speaking of little sisters . . .

The Lower East Side was one of those lucky New York neighborhoods that had been cool forever but was just out of the way and dirty enough to remain free of tourists and Starbucks, and to resist becoming the trendy neighborhood of the moment like the Meatpacking District had become. A line of girls in halter tops and pleated miniskirts and guys in jeans and polo shirts with the collars turned up had formed outside Funktion, the Orchard Street club where the Raves were performing.

Jenny gripped Elise's elbow, gloating inwardly at how cool it was not to have to wait on line with the others, worrying about whether or not the bouncer would let them in. She gave him her name, the velvet rope parted, and in they went.

Ta-da! Instant coolness.

Inside, Funktion was smaller than Jenny had envisioned, and even though it was new, it felt old. The club's floor was painted black and the walls were made of cement blocks painted red. It was crowded, and instead of sitting at the black-and-white checkerboard tables, people crowded near the stage, standing up with beers in hand. The coolest and corniest thing about the club was the fireman's pole left over from when it had been a firehouse. The pole descended center stage from the ceiling, providing a dramatic entrance for whoever was performing.

Jenny wondered if they should brave the bar and order drinks, or if they would have more luck if they just sat down, looking bored and sophisticated until a cocktail waitress came and took their order. Maybe they didn't need to drink at all. Every girl over the age of nine and under the age of twenty-nine was in love with the Raves. Just being in the same room with them, *live*, would be intoxicating enough.

She tugged on the strap of Elise's black-sequined Banana Republic purse and led the way to the back of the club so they could sit down and focus on looking drunkenly bored, like the fashion models always look in those candid pictures in the front pages of *New York* magazine.

The Raves' drummer and bassist were already onstage, fiddling with their instruments and testing mikes.

"*A, B, C, D, E, F, G,*" the drummer sang into his mike, his eyes closed and his face earnest, like he was singing the most heart-wrenching song ever written. "*Tell me what you think of meeeee.*"

"He's cute!" Jenny whispered in Elise's ear.

"Who?" Elise demanded, peering at the stage. "The drummer? But he's, like, twenty-five years old!"

So?

"So?" Jenny retorted. "Aren't they all twenty-five?"

"But he's wearing *overalls*." Elise wrinkled her freckled nose in disgust. "The guitarist, whatsisname . . . Damon . . . no, *Damian* . . . the one Serena's dating? He's the cute one," she insisted. "He has freckles like me, and that *accent*!" she gushed. "And don't forget your brother. *He's* not twenty-five."

Jenny rolled her eyes. Okay, so the drummer *was* wearing

white painter's overalls, with a pink-and-Kelly-green-striped polo shirt and new white Tretorn tennis shoes. It was a bizarrely innocent and preppy outfit for someone famous for breaking his drumsticks against his forehead during concerts. But that was part of his appeal, part of the whole band's appeal. The Raves were a perfect mixture of psychotic serial killer and loveable goofball mama's boy, like Marilyn Manson crossed with the scarecrow from *The Wizard of Oz*.

"I like him," Jenny insisted. She adjusted her chair so she was looking directly at the drummer. He winked in her direction and she giggled, blushing furiously.

"A lotta pretty girls here tonight," the drummer drawled into his mike and then grinned right at Jenny. He had straight white teeth and a wide mouth, like the Cheshire Cat, and his dark hair was short and neatly combed, like he'd just come from that old barber shop on Eighty-third and Lexington where all the little Upper East Side boys go with their dads for their first haircuts.

"He reminds me of the fat guy from that movie," Elise observed, as if anyone would understand who she was talking about.

"He's not fat," Jenny shot back.

Elise pulled an unopened pack of Marlboro Lights out of her sparkly purse and threw them on the table. "You can't really tell if someone's fat until you see them naked."

Jenny considered this as she stared at the drummer. She didn't even know his name, but she liked him. She just did. And she wouldn't have minded seeing him naked. After all, the total number of boys she'd seen completely naked in her lifetime added up to what—zero?

The club was filling up. Jenny even recognized a few people from the line outside who'd finally made it in. All of a sudden the lights went out, except for a single bare bulb illuminating the fireman's pole. Jenny grabbed Elise's hand underneath the table and squeezed it hard, barely able to contain her excitement. Then Damian, the Raves' lead guitarist, slid down the pole, his reddish blond hair sticking straight up like he'd slept on it funny. He was wearing a plain white T-shirt with a big black capital R on the front of it—the Raves' new promo T-shirt, which he'd designed himself.

If you could call that a *design*.

The thing about the Raves was they could get away with wearing anything they wanted or doing anything they pleased because they were true Thoroughbreds—good kids from good Upper East Side families who'd gone to boarding school together and then formed a band instead of going to college. A few months back, *Rolling Stone* had even printed a piece describing how every member of the Raves had gotten into Princeton and how one fateful May night before graduating from boarding school, when they were performing in a Deerfield coffeehouse, a kid in the audience had just happened to be on the phone with his record executive dad, who'd signed them right then and there. The four boys decided not to go to college at all, because what better way to thank your parents for giving you everything you ever wanted than to buy your own car and your own house before the age of twenty? In the end, being rock stars would be much more profitable then getting a college degree in some completely useless subject like philosophy. Plus, the same record executive happened to be married to the director of a French modeling agency, which meant the band could hang out with beautiful French models all the time—a pretty decent perk.

Jenny looked on anxiously as Dan slid down the pole after Damian, landing painfully on his knees. His face was green, his hair was clumpy with sweat, and his eyes were sort of rolling back in his head. He was also dressed like Mr. Way Into Hip-Hop, which totally clashed with the other Raves' grown-up-prep-school-boy ensembles.

"What's with the pants?" Elise asked, looking alarmed, as if she couldn't quite believe that she'd once allowed Dan to kiss her. "And what's with the hair?"

Jenny shrugged her shoulders. She had to admit Dan looked kind of weird, but she would so much rather make goo-goo eyes at the Raves' drummer than try to deconstruct why her brother was suddenly trying to look like Eminem. The drummer smiled at her again and she batted her eyes, wishing her eyelashes were longer or that she'd worn more mascara. She also wished she had the nerve to go up to the bar and ask the bartender to buy the drummer a shot or something. It seemed like the kind of thing Serena would do. If only Serena were there. Or maybe it was best that she wasn't. After all, the drummer was smiling at *her*. If Serena had been there, Jenny might have gone unnoticed.

The crowd was noisy now and seemed to have doubled in size. Elise lit a cigarette and passed it to Jenny. No one had even offered to bring them drinks, but smoking in a room full of legal adults when you were only fourteen felt cool enough.

Damian twanged his guitar and the drummer banged out a drumroll. The anorexic, dark-haired bassist cracked his knuckles. Dan cleared his throat right into the microphone, a disgusting, phlegmy sound.

Gross.

"I guess I should start singing," he mumbled almost incoherently. The crowd tittered. Jenny thought Dan sounded exactly like he did the morning he'd woken up to find they'd run out of instant coffee and he'd become so weak he'd puked. Jenny had had to run out to the deli, and it had taken four cups to revive him. She cocked her head to one side, inhaled, and blew a long stream of smoke into the air. Maybe he was just pretending to be out of it so everyone would be surprised when he started going nuts like he had at Vanessa's birthday party.

Or maybe not.

even v can't watch this train wreck

Beverly was waiting for Vanessa outside the club, wearing the same loose black pants and orange rubber flip-flops as yesterday. His black hair was parted down the middle and his pale blue eyes were shaded by small, round mirrored sunglasses. Very John Lennon meets Keanu Reeves.

"Hi," Vanessa greeted him, hoping she didn't seem *too* excited to see him again. "Nice glasses."

Love the lip ring. You smell fantastic, she willed him to say in response. *And with all certainty, I've decided to move in with you.*

"Should we go in?" was all he asked instead.

The band had already started to play and the line outside the club had dwindled. Vanessa went straight to the front. "Abrams. I'm on the guest list," she told the bouncer. All of a sudden it occurred to her that Dan was about to see her with another guy for the very first time. If only she had the nerve to grab Beverly and make out with him right in front of the stage.

As if Dan would even notice.

The bouncer gave them the once-over and then unhooked the red velvet rope. Vanessa could hear people on line behind them moaning jealously as they went inside. Beverly didn't say anything, as if cool things like that happened to him every day.

Funktion was loud and crowded and smoky and hot, just the way clubs are supposed to be. The Raves were playing with their usual bravado, but the audience seemed to be singing louder than Dan was. Vanessa couldn't even see him yet, but it almost sounded like Dan was choking on something.

Crack me like an egg!
Burn a hole in my finger 'til I find myself
Find myself losing you!
Losing you and missing stuff
Missing how you kicked my ass*!*

Whoa, that song wouldn't be autobiographical, would it?

It was a new song, one that Dan had written only last week. Somehow the hard-core Raves fans had bootlegged a version from one of their practice sessions and had already memorized the lyrics. Now they were shouting them out, which was a good thing, because Dan was barely audible.

Vanessa eased her way through the tightly packed crowd to the back of the club. Dan's little sister Jenny and her friend Elise were seated at a table in the corner, smoking cigarettes and nodding their chins to the music with such studied boredom it was almost obvious they'd been practicing in front of a mirror.

Beverly pointed to a table near the fire exit where there was one free seat. "Go ahead," he told Vanessa. He perched on the table and indicated that she should have the seat. "I'm not sure how much more of this I can take."

Vanessa pressed her lips together and sat down. What was

that supposed to mean? That he didn't like her? That he didn't want to live with her? This wasn't what she'd imagined. They were supposed to sit together in an intimate corner, accidentally knocking knees and touching elbows and getting more and more into each other, all the while pretending to listen to Dan sing.

But maybe that was part of the problem. Dan wasn't singing at all, only the audience was.

Do you miss me? Do I miss you?
I know, I know.
That's not the fucking point.
We were kinda like mowing the grass—
Looked good, smelled good
But such a pain in the ass!

Dan clutched his stomach, gasping into the mike, which he held in white-knuckled fists, his eyes red-rimmed and his sorry mouth gaping like a dying fish's. A fish dressed like the king of *MTV Raps*, in weird baggy pants and ugly sneakers, his hair all sweaty and gross and his neck shaved unevenly.

See what happens to you when we break up? Vanessa thought for a fleeting, gloating moment. Then again, Dan looked so pathetic it was almost embarrassing to admit she even knew him. She glanced at Beverly. He was biting his cuticles and wiggling his foot like someone waiting for a bus.

All of a sudden the distinctive sound of vomit rising to the surface blared over the speakers and Dan staggered offstage, taking the microphone with him. The band continued to play even louder still, with Dan retching miserably in the background.

Way gross.

Vanessa touched Beverly's elbow. "Maybe we should go," she offered apologetically. It felt sort of wrong to leave Dan retching backstage when they'd once been so close, but then again, *he* was the one who wanted to be a rock star. Besides, there was probably a gang of hot blond Raves groupies mopping Dan's head with a cool, damp towel and spoon-feeding him mineral water at that very moment. He didn't need her anymore.

Beverly nodded and slipped off the table. "There's this party my Pratt friends are putting on that's been going on since March. Let's check it out."

He held out his hand, and Vanessa noticed for the first time that he was missing the last joint on the middle finger of his left hand.

Ew!?!

She tried not to stare and allowed him to pull her to her feet. If only Dan would come back onstage long enough to see her leaving with another guy. But the club was way too crowded for ex-girlfriend sightings, and besides, Dan was otherwise occupied.

Again the sound of his retching came over the speakers, nearly drowning out the music.

A little advice, dude: We all know how attached you are to that mike, but next time you're gonna hurl, please leave it behind?!

better in translation

Luckily for Dan, Damian and the other members of the band had enough confidence and humor not to get all uptight about the fact that their new lead singer was puking his guts out a few feet offstage. They played right through Dan's little episode, subtly cut the sound to his mike, and then segued into an old Raves song that Dan had never even heard before:

Babycakes, you make my eyes scream
Lick the drips, then toss the cone a-waaayee

No wonder they were looking for a songwriter.

The crowd went wild, singing the words with more passion than ever. Dan remained offstage with his head between his knees, trying to remember how he'd gotten himself into this situation in the first place. How on earth had he gone from reclusive high-school poet to the baggy-pants-wearing front man of a famous band when he so obviously lacked the mettle for it?

Before the gig started, he'd done what Damian suggested and drunk some vodka. Okay—he'd drunk close to half the bottle, but instead of relaxing him or giving him the courage to perform, it had made him feel totally toxic, especially when combined with an entire pack of cigarettes.

Well, *duh*!

The light was dim backstage, and the wooden floor was sticky with spilled beer and cigarette ash. Dan gritted his teeth as another wave of nausea gripped him, but he squeezed his eyes shut and fought it off. Suddenly someone tapped him on the shoulder. "Eet's all right, *mon cher*. 'Ave a seep of tonique et voilà—you are all better, yeah?"

Dan looked up to find a gorgeous girl in her early twenties standing over him with a little bottle of Schweppes tonic water and a glass of ice in her hands. She poured the tonic over the ice and squatted down beside him.

"Here. No lime, yeah?"

Dan didn't know what to say. He'd never drunk tonic without vodka, but at this point he'd try anything. The girl had long honey-colored hair and was deeply tanned. She was wearing a tight white tank top and a swishy green skirt that barely covered the tops of her long, tan thighs. Her eyes were olive green and she smelled kind of like pine nuts. He took the glass and put it to his lips, taking a tiny, tentative sip. It would be just his luck for the sip to backfire on him, spewing all over the girl's beautiful hair. Miraculously, though, it didn't. He took another sip, and then another, and with each sip, his head cleared ever so slightly.

"Zat's enough," the girl told him firmly, and took the glass away. She put it and the empty bottle on top of an unused amp and turned back to Dan. "When zee boyz are fineeshed, they vill make a party," she continued, her olive green eyes sleepy and confident. "And zen we vill talk."

Dan nodded obediently, as if she was making complete sense. He was pretty sure the girl was French, and when she said, "And zen we vill talk," it almost sounded like she had more than a little polite chit-chat in mind. But how could she possibly find him attractive in his current state? Maybe his performance translated better in another language.

The girl stood in the wings, watching the band finish up their song. "Zey will play two more songs *et puis finis*, yeah?" she declared.

Dan nodded again. That sounded about right. A tattoo encircled the girl's tanned ankle. At first glance Dan thought the tattoo was of a snake; then he realized it was of a fox, curled around her leg, asleep.

Oh, the poems he could write about that fox if only he had a pen, a notebook, and a large container of extra-strength Advil!

He cleared his cigarette-abused throat. "I'm Dan," he croaked, extending his hand but not daring to stand up.

The girl smiled, a sexy little gap appearing between her front teeth. Then she walked over, grasped his clammy hand, and bent down to kiss his clammy cheek. "I know who you are," she murmured breathily into his ear. *"Et je m'appelle Monique."*

Hmmm, Dan mused drunkenly. Was there even a word for *foxy* in French?

yale loves new york

Stanford Parris III lived in the penthouse at 1000 Park Avenue in Carnegie Hill, one of the oldest and most elegant doorman buildings on the Upper East Side. But Mr. Parris's Chippendale furniture, medieval tapestries, and eighteenth-century British sculpture collection went unnoticed by most of the guests, including the van der Woodsens. They were used to such elegance, and it only made them feel more at home.

"My grandson wanted me to have the party at a hotel," Stanford Parris III confided to Mr. van der Woodsen as he shook his hand. "Or at the Yacht Club." He winked at Serena's mother. "But I wasn't about to pass up an opportunity to host so many beautiful women in my own home!"

Serena's mother smiled her gracious you-can-say-anything-to-me-you-old-lech-and-I'll-never-lose-my-poise smile, and Serena giggled. Maybe old Stan Parris wasn't so bad after all. She shook the ancient New England aristocrat's hand and then stood on tiptoe and planted a flirtatious kiss on his withered old cheek just to piss her parents off.

"I say," Mr. Parris exclaimed. "Yale certainly knows what it's doing!"

"Easy, Granddad," warned a tall blond boy with an adorable dimple in his chin and amazing cheekbones. "Remember, you have a bad heart," the boy scolded his grandfather.

"It's not *my* heart I'm worried about," Mr. Parris grumbled. He clasped the boy on the shoulder with a wrinkled hand. "Miss Serena van der Woodsen, this is my grandson, Stanford Parris the Fifth."

Like anyone actually cares how many Stanford Parrises there are?

Serena waited for the boy to blush with embarrassment and mutter something about how plain old "Stan" would be just fine, but he didn't. Obviously he thought his title was the best thing ever. What did they call him at school? she wondered. Number Five? Stan 5?

"Here's your nametag, dear." Serena's mother pasted a bumper-sticker-sized white nametag with *Serena van der Woodsen, Incoming Fall* written on it in blue marker over Serena's breasts, like some sort of hideous, adhesive-backed tube top.

Serena pretended not to mind. "Thanks, Mom," she said, cupping her hands over her chest to smooth out the nametag. Every male present let out a little gasp, all getting psyched for Yale's coed dorms next year.

They were early and the party was thin. Boys in Hugo Boss suits and ties and girls in long Tocca skirts and buttoned-up blouses lurked by their parents' sides, smiling awkwardly and guzzling champagne. The whole scene made Serena feel like she was at her first day of ballroom dancing class, back in fifth grade.

Someone tapped Serena on the shoulder and she turned around. It was Mrs. Archibald, Nate's dramatic, French, slightly crazy mother. Her dyed amber hair had been blown out into a mass of cascading curls, and her thin lips were painted a fierce fire-engine red. Around her neck were six strands of rose-colored pearls, and matching rose-colored pearls punctuated each ear. Despite her three-inch Christian Louboutin heels, she was surprisingly tiny, dressed in a sleek, pewter-colored strapless Oscar de la Renta silk evening gown and carrying a little gold satchel and gold opera glasses— obviously just stopping by at the party on her way to the theater. She kissed Serena quickly on both cheeks. "Have you seen my son?" she whispered in Serena's ear, her green eyes flashing.

Serena shook her head. "No. But Blair's—" She stopped short, wondering if Mrs. Archibald really wanted to know that Blair and Nate were holed up in a Plaza Hotel suite, having lots of sex. "Have you tried his cell?" she asked instead.

Mrs. Archibald batted her eyelashes and waved her opera glasses in the air. "Never mind, darling," she sighed, before rustling off to find her husband, the admiral.

Stan 5 was still standing by as if it were only right that the handsomest blond guy and the most beautiful blond girl in the room should be talking to each other. A woman in a black caterer's uniform handed Serena a flute of champagne. "Where's *your* nametag?" Serena asked Stan 5, scanning his black oxford-cloth shirt that had been left unbuttoned and tieless.

What a rebel.

He grinned and cleared his throat. "I didn't think I needed one."

Oh, so like everyone is just supposed to *know* who you are?

Serena was ready to ditch the party already—she'd shown

up and stayed ten minutes, what more did her parents want? But then old Mr. Parris shuffled over to talk to her again, and she didn't want to be rude.

"Your mother was just telling me what a wonderful actress you are," he boomed in his charming New England accent. He adjusted his burgundy-and-navy-blue-striped bow tie. "You know, I played the lead in nineteen productions back when I was a Yalie. The school was men-only in those days. I've got some old pictures if you'd like to take a look."

"Honestly, Granddad," Stan 5 huffed in an effort to shut his grandfather up.

"Actually, I'd love to," Serena replied with genuine interest. There was nothing she liked better than to look at old pictures. She loved the elaborate clothes, the dramatic bouffant hairstyles, the way everyone wore hats and gloves and handbags that matched their shoes.

Stan 5 frowned in confusion, as if he couldn't believe Serena was about to ditch him for his wrinkly old grandfather. She flashed him the same gracious smile her mom had flashed his grandfather, and then followed the elder Mr. Parris through the apartment and down a narrow corridor to his library. His right leg seemed to be giving him trouble, causing him to list to the left, and she gripped the elbow of his dapper gray pinstriped blazer for fear he would fall.

The Parris library was decorated in chocolate brown with hints of navy blue and gold fleur-de-lys. Three crystal chandeliers hung from the ceiling, and four chocolate brown leather club chairs stood around an ornately painted antique card table.

"There I am in *Hamlet*." Mr. Parris pointed to a large black-and-white photograph hanging over the mantel. Serena expected to see a young Mr. Parris in a full suit of armor, looking fierce and haughty. Instead, a beautiful young girl with a long thin face and a distinctive cleft in her chin lay with her long-lashed eyes closed and her hands folded across her chest, a chain of daisies entwined in her loose fair hair.

"That's *you*?" Serena asked in amazement.

The old man chuckled. "I was a pretty boy back then. They made me play Ophelia."

Serena stared at the photograph. "You were kind of hot."

Mr. Parris patted her hand. "I like to think so. And I was so much better at dying than the other fellows." He went over to the wet bar in the corner, filled two crystal tumblers full of scotch, and set them on the card table. Then he pulled a worn green leather-bound album off the bookshelf. He flipped through the pages of the album and pointed to one of the leather club chairs. "I've got hundreds of photographs," he warned Serena.

Serena sat down and took a sip of scotch. Then she scooted back in her chair, tucked her feet up underneath her, and reached for the album. She felt cozy and comfortable and genuinely interested in looking at Stanford Parris III's old Yale pictures. And as she slowly turned the pages, examining the wonderful black-and-white images of a young Mr. Parris and his handsome Yale acting buddies rehearsing onstage, she realized she hadn't really thought about acting *at* college. She could even imagine playing Ophelia just like Mr. Parris had, fluttering her eyes closed and folding up like a flower when it was time to die.

"Here I am in *Kiss Me Kate*." Mr. Parris pointed to a photograph of the same long-faced beauty glaring at the camera, her dark eyes flashing, her cleft chin raised disdainfully. "What a witch, that Kate."

Serena studied the photograph. Mr. Parris as Kate reminded her of someone she knew, but she just couldn't place her.

Let's give her a hint. Her first name starts with *B*.

She continued to flip through the photographs, her mind racing. Yale was the only school that hadn't stalked her with perky e-mails and overzealous fan mail. Even the Whiffenpoofs—Yale's all-male a capella singing troupe, whom she'd met last month, had the decency not to e-mail her every day asking her when she was planning to arrive on campus so they could help her with her bags or take her out for coffee or whatever. And they certainly hadn't asked her about Damian from the Raves, whom she'd never even met.

Mr. Parris tapped Serena on the knee. "You have the face of a leading lady," he added. "Yale knows what they're doing."

"You think so?" Serena replied enthusiastically. Suddenly, ditching the Yale party to check out the Raves concert seemed totally unnecessary. And out of respect for old Mr. Parris, she almost wished she'd actually worn the entire gray-and-blue outfit her mom had laid out on her bed. She was going to be Yale University's greatest leading lady since Stanford Parris III. New Haven was so close to New York, she could still model, and with a bit more acting experience under her belt, she might even get a film deal! Blair would be totally thrilled if they went to school together—not that she was going to say anything until Blair found out she was off Yale's wait list. Blair could be kind of unreasonable when Serena had something she wanted for herself.

Kind of?!

party crasher finds kindred spirit

"Brave soul." A tall blond boy wearing an open-collared black oxford-cloth shirt greeted Blair as she stepped off the elevator alone and into Stanford Parris III's country club of an apartment. "Everyone else was dragged here by their parents. One guy even bagged, so his parents had to come alone."

Wonder who *that* was?

"I'm Stanford Parris the Fifth, by the way." The boy extended his hand and flashed her a proud smile that seemed to say, "As if you didn't know that."

Blair grinned back. She loved boys with titles, especially tall blond ones with cute dimples in their chins, and especially ones who were going to Yale next year. "Blair Waldorf," she said, shaking his hand. She fingered the custom-engraved Cartier pendant at her throat—the very same one she'd stolen from her baby sister. It was a simple nameplate, just the word *Yale* in gold cursive, tied with a light blue satin ribbon around her neck. "So where are your parents?" she demanded.

"In Scotland. We have a castle there," Stan 5 boasted casually.

Blair giggled. "So do we! My aunt lives there."

Aw, isn't that cute? If they got married and honeymooned in Scotland, they could go castle-hopping!

"Anyway, this is Granddad's party. I'm just here to . . ." Stan 5 paused and cleared his throat, as if he'd momentarily forgotten why he was there. Or maybe he'd just drunk too much scotch. "To get our class excited for next year," he explained finally.

Blair rubbed her well-glossed lips together. Stanford Parris's grandson. She'd stumbled upon the youngest member of one of Yale's most influential alumnae families without even trying! If anyone could get her off the wait list and into Yale, *he* could.

Stan 5 pointed to the Yale pendant at her throat. "That's unusual," he observed. "Guess you're really excited about next year, huh?"

That's one way of putting it.

Blair blushed fiercely. She had prepared herself for this sort of question. "My parents had it made for me right after I found out I was in," was what she'd planned on saying. But now she opted for the truth. She stood on tiptoe and cupped her hand around Stan 5's aristocratic ear. "I'm not actually in yet," she whispered. "I got wait-listed."

"Well, we'll just have to see what we can do about that," Stan 5 chuckled sympathetically. He snatched two flutes of champagne off a passing tray and handed her one. They clinked glasses and a little thrill ran up Blair's spine. She was about to get lucky, she could just tell.

In more ways than one!

Suddenly there was a rustle of tulle and Nate's mother enveloped her in a Chanel No. 5–soaked embrace. "Darling, where is Nate?" Mrs. Archibald demanded in her dramatic, Anglo-French accent.

Good question.

Blair didn't want to have to explain to Stan 5 who Nate was, and she didn't want Nate's mom to think she couldn't keep track of her own boyfriend. But she also didn't want her to suspect that she was hiding something. After all, she was dying to find out where Nate was too—so she could kick the shit out of him.

"I've been staying at the Plaza, so I haven't had a chance to check my messages at home," she responded vaguely. "I think maybe his cell phone broke or something, because he never answers."

"I know." Mrs. Archibald pursed her fiery red lipsticked lips. "The gardener found his cell phone on the roof." She raised her severely penciled eyebrows suspiciously. "You are sure he is not staying at the Plaza with you?"

Blair glanced self-consciously at Stan 5 and then shook her head, refusing to answer the question out loud. How embarrassing to have to admit to your boyfriend's mom that actually no, you hadn't managed to lock him up in a hotel room for days of wild, passionate sex. In fact, that plan had totally backfired.

"Well then." Mrs. Archibald kissed her on both cheeks and smiled tightly as if to say, "I don't believe a word you're saying, but I'm late for the opera, so c'est la vie."

"If you *do* see him, darling, tell him his mother and father are quite cross with him, and have gone to *La Bohème*."

Blair clasped her hands behind her back and nodded dutifully. Where the fuck *was* Nate anyway? She watched Nate's father help Mrs. Archibald on with her beaded silk Oscar de la Renta capelet and then escort her to the elevator. She thought of going over to say hello, but Admiral Archibald was famous for his bad temper, and if he was angry with Nate, it was probably best to stay out of his way.

Besides, she had more important things to do. Like flirt with Mr. I-Can-Get-You-Into-Yale the Fifth.

Blair noticed that he was wearing what looked like an antique Yale insignia ring. "It's my granddad's," Stan 5 explained. "He gave it to me when I got in. Yale is like Granddad's whole life. I'd introduce you, but he disappeared into his study with this beautiful blond girl, and who knows when they'll come out. Not that he's a pervert or anything. He's probably just boring her to death with his Yale stories."

Blair's eyes swept the room. The "beautiful blond girl" sounded suspiciously like Serena. Old Mr. Parris was an actual trustee of Yale, and far more influential than his grandson. How typical of Serena to monopolize the one person in the room who could probably get her into Yale once and for all.

A man in a catering uniform took their empty champagne glasses and handed them each a fresh one.

"To Yale," Stan 5 said, before clinking his glass against hers.

Blair fingered the pendant around her neck and downed her drink, wondering if she should demand an introduction to his grandfather. Stan 5 took a step toward her and lowered his aristocratic chin. "Don't worry," he murmured reassuringly, as if reading her mind. "Granddad and I are very close."

Blair clutched the stem of her champagne flute and batted her eyelashes, willing her face not to flush too retardedly red. How lucky she was to have nabbed the younger, hotter Stanford Parris while Serena was stuck with the old moldy one!

"I kissed my Yale interviewer," she confided before she could stop herself. It wasn't exactly something she was proud of. But she wanted Stan 5 to know what he was up against.

Stan 5 smiled delightedly. "Granddad keeps a room for me down the hall. I've got his whole collection of vintage Yale catalogs in there. Want to take a look?"

Blair giggled giddily. How wonderful to meet a boy who was as crazily enthusiastic about Yale as she was. Eagerly, she followed Stan 5 into his room. She couldn't wait to kiss his catalogs.

Kiss?

Why not, when she had more in common with Stanford Parris V than she did with any other boy she'd ever met, including her lame-ass, no-show boyfriend, who was already into Yale anyway and was totally unsympathetic and useless?

Well, then. Guess she meant *kiss* after all.

n abandons ship

"Oops, I think I'm winning." Lexie giggled and popped another Oreo half into her mouth.

"Nice one," Nate responded, not even trying to fend off her chocolaty lips.

It had been Lexie's idea to smoke another joint and play checkers with Oreos, so she'd made up the rules: Every time she nabbed one of Nate's white-faced Oreo halves with her whole Oreos, she got to eat the Oreo half and kiss Nate on the lips.

Nate really wasn't that into the game, which meant he was sort of letting Lexie win, but kissing her on deck where everyone else was hanging out seemed safer than sitting alone with her up in the crow's nest where one thing could have led to another and . . .

Not that he would have actually let anything *major* happen. Right?

As usual, Nate was suffering from the Curse of Blair. Whenever he fooled around with another girl, all he could think about was Blair and fooling around with Blair, making him feel sort of guilty and horny at the same time, which made it simultaneously kind of hard to take and kind of hard to stop.

He kept his eyes open as Lexie kissed him, making eye contact with Jeremy on the other side of the deck, who was kissing some girl with long brown hair and fat arms whom Nate had never seen before. All of a sudden Nate felt like he was in seventh grade at one of those parties where everyone just lay around kissing because they thought that was what they were supposed to do, even though it was kind of nasty to suck on some girl's tongue for like, an hour, without having a drink of water or anything. Except for that time with Blair in Serena's closet at a party back in eighth grade—or was it sixth? They'd kissed and talked for so long Serena had had to drag them out so they wouldn't miss the entire party. If only Blair would suddenly draw up alongside the *Charlotte* in a little dinghy and shout up at him to grow the fuck up in that sexy, bitchy tone she used when she was only mildly infuriated with him. Where *was* Blair anyway? he wondered in stoned, sleepless confusion. Why wasn't she with him?

Hello? Anyone home? Wake up!!!

Lexie had her eyes closed and was breathing heavily as she sucked on his lips. Her tongue tasted like chocolate and beer, which was kind of a bad combination. Nate could hardly wait to push her off his lap and head belowdecks to gulp a few glasses of cold water. He could also hardly wait to tell Blair that despite this bumpy little interlude everything would turn out all right once he got back from Bermuda, or New Jersey, or wherever the fuck they were headed.

His gaze shifted to the starboard side of the boat. The sun was going down, and they'd finally made it into the ocean. The dark water was quiet and a few fishing boats twinkled on the horizon. Nate hadn't checked the boat's navigational system in a few hours. The *Charlotte* had been cruising on autopilot ever since they'd headed out, but since he was the only one who knew how to sail her and was kind of responsible for the safety of everyone onboard, he thought maybe he'd better check it out.

Yeah, maybe.

He pulled away from Lexie and whispered hoarsely into her ear. "I gotta go steer the boat."

She slid off his lap, popped another Oreo into her mouth, and gave his bicep a squeeze. "Vhat a stud. You know, I always vanted to go to Ber-mooda."

Nate headed aft to the captain's cabin, stepping over the prone bodies of his stoned, drunk, and half-asleep shipmates. Some kid from his world religion class was wearing one of the *Charlotte*'s orange life vests while he played the harmonica and sang an old Neil Young tune:

Helpless, helpless, helpless, helpless.

Nate was creepily reminded of the movie *Titanic*—which Blair had made him watch not once but four times—right before the boat sinks.

Charlie and Anthony had locked themselves into the cabin and were sitting cross-legged on the floor, sharing a bong. They'd taken off their shirts and were trying to see who could stick his stomach out the farthest—a ridiculous contest, since both their stomachs were so flat they verged on concave.

"Hey," Anthony greeted Nate. "We were wondering—is there surfing in Bermuda?"

"Because we should have brought our boards," Charlie added.

Nate shook his head, ignoring them. The air in the cabin was so full of smoke he could barely read the monitors. From what he could tell, though, they were nearing Cape May, which meant that if they traveled at a normal cruising speed instead of .5 miles an hour, it would only take a little over three hours to get back to New York Harbor. He'd dock the boat and head straight for the Plaza.

Only a whole day late.

Nate checked the incoming messages screen where the *Charlotte* picked up text messages—mostly communication from other boats or ports. There were thirty-seven text messages from AdArch@nextel.net, his father's cell phone.

NATHANIEL, YOUR MOTHER AND I ARE AT THE OPERA.

NATHANIEL, TURN THE BOAT AROUND.

I'VE ALERTED THE COAST GUARD AND THEY'VE BEEN INSTRUCTED TO ARREST YOU.

NATHANIEL, YOUR MOTHER IS VERY UPSET.

TURN THE BOAT AROUND, SON.

And so on.

"Shit." Nate could imagine his mother crying in her black evening attire in their box at the Metropolitan Opera while his father stabbed furiously at his cell phone. Then again, his mother always cried at the opera; it was part of her whole dramatic-French-princess act.

The messages had all been sent within the last two hours, so it wasn't like his parents had been freaking out for that long. Normally his father's surly tone would have scared the crap out of him, but he'd been looking for an excuse to abort the mission and get back to Blair. Now here it was.

He went back to the navigation screen and punched in the longitudinal and latitudinal points for the harbor at Battery Park City, which were written on the blackboard on the wall of the cabin in yellow chalk. He hit enter and immediately the boat's motor shifted into neutral. Then the bow dipped and swung around until the boat had done a complete hundred-and-eighty-degree turn back in the direction of New York Harbor. He typed the command to increase speed to thirty-three miles per hour and glanced at the clock: 8:29 P.M. He'd be back in bed with Blair by midnight.

"Yo, what's up, dude?" Anthony demanded from his spot on the cabin floor. "Are you doing homework or something?"

Nate grinned and shook his head, enjoying the buzz from their secondhand smoke. Blair would be so thrilled to see him again she'd have to forgive him. And he wouldn't have any trouble making her forget.

Presuming she was there waiting for him. And presuming she was alone . . .

twisted little sister

"Remove your shoes! Remove your shoes! Ree-moove your shoo-oo-ooes!" Damian screeched into the mike. It was the final chorus of "Japanese Restaurant," the latest hit single written by Dan Humphrey and the last song on the Raves' playlist.

"If we slip out now," Elise murmured, "we can probably get a cab before anyone else."

Who said anything about leaving?

Jenny lit another cigarette, ignoring her. She wanted to hang out until the crowd thinned, and get a better look at Damian. See if his red-blond hair stood up on end all on its own or if it was crusty with hair gel. See if his teeth were really as perfectly white and straight as they looked from where she sat. Hear that Irish twang he was so famous for. And those arm muscles! The Raves' drummer was still cute, but she had to admit Damian was totally hot. He had this incredible energy about him, like he'd been wound up. If she stuck around, maybe Dan would even introduce them, and she could casually slip in that she was friends with Serena, and find out if they were actually together or not.

That is, if Dan was still alive.

Zoing! Damian struck the last chord on his guitar and

threw his instrument into the crowd, as he was known to do. Then he climbed up the fireman's pole hand-over-hand, flexing those fantastic arm muscles, and disappeared.

"Show-off," the drummer scoffed. He stood up stiffly, grabbed a bottle of beer from beneath his drum set, and chugged it. Then he set the bottle down and craned his neck, like he was looking for someone in the crowd.

Jenny's skin tingled. *Her?*

Wait, wasn't she over him already?

"We should get going," Elise repeated. She stood up and tugged on her shirt. "Everyone's going to be fighting for cabs."

The bassist started unplugging things and breaking down the equipment. The drummer burped irreverently into one of the mikes.

Gross.

Jenny giggled like this was the handsomest, most adorable thing she'd ever heard.

"You can go if you want, but I'm not leaving," she told her friend. She was supposed to spend the rest of the weekend at Elise's house, but opportunities like this didn't present themselves very often.

Opportunities to meet the famous rock stars, or opportunities to be as naughty as possible?

The crowd began to disperse. Some headed to the bathrooms; others spilled out the exit doors and onto the street. Elise hovered next to the table, unsure. Jenny took another awkward puff on her cigarette and jiggled her foot. And then all of a sudden he was there, in front of them—the drummer.

He wasn't Damian, but he was *almost* as good.

"Hey. I'm Lloyd." His knuckles were wrapped in frayed surgical tape like a boxer's, and his dark, neatly cut hair and preppy pink-and-green Lacoste shirt were soaked with perspiration. "You're Dan's sister, Jennifer, right?"

Jenny nodded. She loved it when people called her Jennifer. Although she would have preferred it if he'd said, "You're Jennifer, that stunning model in the *W* spread this month, right?"

"How'd you know?" she asked, even though she knew the answer. Despite the fact that she dressed better than Dan did and was nearly nine inches shorter and had a much bigger chest, they could almost have been fraternal twins.

Except that she was also three years younger than Dan. Not that she was about to tell Mr. Drummer Boy that.

"Your brother said his gorgeous sister was coming," Lloyd replied with a completely straight face. He glanced at Elise, who was still standing there, fidgeting with the zipper on her Banana Republic purse like a total geek. "Marc, our bassist? He's got this thing about big old hotels," Lloyd continued. "Anyway, he's booked some big suite up at the Plaza Hotel. We're having a little get-together there if you want to come."

Jenny let her cigarette fall to the floor. She'd almost forgotten she was holding it. "Totally!" she exclaimed with more enthusiasm than she'd intended. "I mean, my brother's going, right?" Not that she really cared if Dan was going. She just didn't want to sound like the type of girl who partied in hotel rooms with strange guys from rock bands all the time.

Right.

"It's ten minutes till my curfew. I have to get home," Elise insisted. She gave Jenny a look as if to say, "This is your last chance."

"Okay. Well, I'll call you tomorrow," Jenny responded. She handed Elise the pack of cigarettes, but Elise waved them away.

"You might need them," she said, before turning to go.

Jenny knew she ought to have felt a twinge of guilt for not leaving with her friend, but how could she pass up a chance like this? The worst thing that could happen was that her father would find out, but he'd never been very good at punishments, and besides, Elise would never tell. She squeezed her knees together and smiled up at Lloyd with nervous excitement. He held out a bandaged hand and pulled her to her feet.

"Come on. I'll introduce you around."

The club had returned to a state of normalcy. People chatted quietly over their beers while the new Franz Ferdinand album played on the stereo. Dan was sitting on the edge of the stage now, next to a very pretty tanned girl with honey-colored hair, cradling a bottle of Schweppes tonic water. He looked completely spent, but the girl was chattering away, laughing and smiling like Dan was the most entertaining guy she'd ever met.

"Fucking hell, Yoko's back," Lloyd hissed under his breath as they approached.

"Who?" Jenny asked curiously. The girl was wearing a supershort tiered jade green miniskirt, and her bare legs were luxuriously long and tanned, like those of a Bain de Soleil sunscreen model.

A giant fake smile spread across Lloyd's face. "Never mind," he responded between gleaming white teeth. "You'll see."

The tanned girl shimmied off the stage and kissed Jenny on both cheeks. "Dan says you are his seeez-stirrh," she said in a thick French accent. "I am so jealous of doz gorgeous bresssts!" She reached out with both hands and gave each of Jenny's boobs a good hard squeeze.

Honk, honk!

"So womanly, *non?*"

"Monique, I wouldn't—" Dan started to warn her.

"Thanks," Jenny interrupted, surprising everyone including herself. She'd always been extremely sensitive about her chest, with good reason, but Monique's little outburst seemed like a genuine French compliment. Besides, she didn't really mind that Damian and Lloyd were now well aware that her boobs were the largest in the room.

"Jennifer, this is Monique. Monique, Jennifer." Lloyd introduced them. "Monique is Dam—"

"Visiting from St. Tropez," Monique cut him off, her eyes burning with a look that had, "Shut up, you idiot!" written all over it. "Are you coming to zee Plaza 'otel wid us?" she asked Jenny.

"No, she has to go home," Dan slurred. "It's late." He glanced around the club with bleary eyes. "Isn't it?"

Well, his outfit was definitely tired.

Little sister lesson number two: Don't even think about telling her what to do.

"No way," Jenny corrected her brother. "I am *so* coming."

Damian slid down the fireman's pole and bounded up to them. He'd changed into an olive green tracksuit with the words JUICE ME smeared on the butt in white paint. "Ready to ruckus, yeah?" he demanded, clapping Dan and Lloyd on their backs.

Monique flashed him a sweet I'm-only-tolerating-you-because-you're-famous sort of smile and hooked her arm possessively through Dan's.

Lloyd grabbed Jenny and squashed her into a sort of three-way bear hug with Damian. "Damian, meet Jennifer. Jennifer, meet Damian."

Jenny was so excited, it was a good thing Lloyd was hugging

her so tight, or she would have collapsed on the floor. Damian made an exaggerated delighted gasping sound, like an overly gay man discovering the cutest little doggie raincoat he'd ever seen. Then he kissed Jenny on the tip of her nose.

So maybe he wasn't Serena's new boyfriend.

"Why don't Danny and Monique take the limo? The rest of us can squeeze into a cab," Damian offered.

"I could sit on someone's lap," Jenny volunteered.

"Of course you can," said Lloyd.

"Of course you can," Damian agreed.

Of course she can.

ain't nobody here but us chickens

"I take more APs than anyone else in my class, and I have an A average," Blair complained.

"Then you should have applied early admission," Stan 5 advised.

"But don't you understand. *I kissed my interviewer*," Blair whispered loudly, sounding like a broken record. "My college advisor said there was no way they'd take me early."

Stan 5 shrugged. "Smaller pool of applicants. Better chance to shine."

Blair gritted her teeth to hold back a volley of expletives. She'd planned on applying to Yale early admission since she was thirteen years old. Why had she listened to clueless, bloody-nosed, wig-wearing Ms. Glos and not trusted her instincts? And why hadn't she met Stan 5 like, a year ago, when he could have been really useful?

They were lying on their stomachs on the double bed in the room Stan 5's grandfather kept for him, and had already thumbed through every Yale catalog since 1947, laughing at the clothes people wore and the corny phrases underneath the photos. Things like, "Here's looking at you, kid!" and "Ain't nobody here but us chickens!" The room was decorated with

Yale paraphernalia: Yale swim team pennants, Stan III's B.A. in English and dramatic arts, a New Haven newspaper article featuring Stan III as one of Yale's most gifted young actors, and a yellow card from the Yale University registrar listing every semester old Stan III had made the dean's list.

"It looks like Yale is your grandfather's whole life," Blair observed. Her shoes were half on, half off, and she bounced them up and down on the ends of her toes.

Stan 5 rolled over and looked up at the ceiling. "Yeah," he answered hollowly.

Blair wasn't sure why he sounded so bummed. After all, Yale was her whole life too, but she was the one still stuck on the wait list.

Stan 5 reached out and twirled a strand of Blair's dark hair around his finger. "We should stop talking about this," he told her, letting the twirl go, "or you're going to get seriously depressed."

"But—" Blair started to say. Exactly when were they going to devise a plan to get her into Yale?

Stan 5 rolled over and grabbed her arms, pulling her toward him. "We should stop talking period," he said, his eyes hungrily searching her face. "Like I said, my grandfather and I are *really* close. So don't worry about getting in, okay?"

This was the part in the movie where the music was supposed to slow down, heads were supposed to meet, and boy and girl were supposed to kiss so passionately that their clothes would wind up in a pile on the floor while the windows steamed up. Stan 5 was going to get her into Yale! But for some reason—maybe it was the quantity of Yale paraphernalia on the walls and all over the floor, or maybe it was because she'd drunk four glasses of champagne at a party she hadn't even been invited to, or maybe it was because kissing any boy other than Nate felt truly naughty—Blair couldn't manage to just close her eyes and kiss Stanford Parris V. All she could do was snort and giggle like a twelve-year-old.

She pushed him away, snorting and giggling so hard she choked.

"What?" Stan 5 asked, pushing himself up on his elbows. His blond hair fell into his eyes and he pushed it away.

Blair snorted again. She felt giddy and confused and very much in need of a little girl talk with Serena. "I don't know." She got up and jammed her feet into her shoes. "Um, I have to go find someone. Maybe I'll see you later?"

Stan 5 seemed to enjoy how hot and bothered she was. He grinned cockily at her and raised his blond eyebrows. "Maybe."

As she left the room, Blair tried to pull herself together.

Not maybe. Definitely.

the women are smarter

"I never really thought of Hamlet as tragic per se," Serena found herself telling Stanford Parris III. She'd only skimmed *Hamlet* when they'd had to write an essay on it for English class, but she'd always been an excellent bullshit artist. Even without reading every word she'd noticed that Hamlet reminded her of Dan Humphrey, who she'd hooked up with earlier in the fall. So woeful and neurotic. "I mean, all he needed was a little Zoloft or something and he'd probably have conquered all of Scandinavia and had, like, a wife in every country."

Well, hello, Miss I Know All There Is to Know About Shakespeare.

Mr. Parris nodded. "Wellbutrin. That's what I take."

Like she really needed to know that.

"I like reading," Serena went on, completely bemused by what was coming out of her mouth. "As long as I have nothing else to do," she corrected herself.

Which was almost never.

"I guess that's the trouble I'm going to have, you know, with picking a major? I won't be able to decide between English and drama." She smiled and pulled her short skirt demurely over her knees.

Since when is the city's biggest party girl worried about her major?

"Elementary, my dear. That's why they invented the double major!" Mr. Parris snapped his suspenders, obviously delighted with the opportunity to divulge his vast wisdom to a young girl of such extraordinary beauty and intelligence.

All of a sudden Blair burst into the room, dressed a little too sexily for an academic gathering and wearing the Yale pendant her mother had ordered from Cartier for baby Yale. Serena had never seen her best friend look so bizarre.

"Thank God I found you!" Blair babbled breathlessly. She glanced at Mr. Parris. "Sorry for interrupting, sir, but this is an emergency!"

Serena could always tell when Blair was up to something or was just plain freaking out, because her nostrils flared like a wild animal and she forgot to blink. Right now she looked like a squirrel with rabies. Serena stood up and shook Mr. Parris's hand. "It was truly a pleasure talking to you, Mr. Parris."

Mr. Parris bent down and kissed her hand. "The pleasure was entirely mine."

Blair coughed. Of course Serena had completely enchanted the old man, which was totally unfair because Blair was the one who actually *needed* to enchant him. "This really is an emergency," she blurted impatiently.

Not exactly enchanting.

"Okay, I'm coming," Serena murmured. She looped her arm through Blair's and Blair dragged her to the front hall and pushed the button for the elevator. "Where are we going anyway?" Serena demanded as the elevator doors rolled open.

"The Plaza!" Blair squealed, dragging her inside.

And it's probably safe to say they weren't going to discuss Shakespeare once they got there.

and you thought andy warhol was dead

Vanessa and Beverly walked up an enclosed ramp that led into the warehouse space in Williamsburg where Beverly's friends' party was taking place. Vanessa could hear music coming from inside—something airy and rhythmic that might have been Björk, although she wasn't sure. A woman pushed open the black metal door at the top of the ramp and stomped past wearing a yellow bandana in her hair, black kneesocks, and fluorescent yellow clogs. She looked like she'd been crying, and was cradling her left hand against her chest.

"Hey, Bethene," Beverly called to her as she stomped away.

"What are those?" Vanessa peered into a bucket of what she hoped were very well produced stuffed animals, sitting on the floor halfway up the ramp.

"Kittens," Beverly replied, as if no further explanation was required.

The ramp seemed to be fashioned as a sort of display, and was scattered with random art objects. Beside the bucket of kittens was a life-sized wax figure of Santa Claus carrying a huge see-through plastic sack full of naked Barbie dolls with their heads missing. At Santa's feet was a lava lamp with real-looking eyeballs floating around inside it. The ramp was like a haunted house, only slightly more disturbing.

Slightly?

"Everyone here is an artist," Beverly declared, "and they've been doing this party since March."

Vanessa nodded, even though she wasn't exactly sure what he meant by "doing this party." It sounded a little like the art "happenings" at Andy Warhol's Factory back in the 1960s— lots of cool arty people collaborating to make weird art that no one really understood and that wasn't even very good.

When they reached the top of the ramp, Beverly pushed the door open and they stepped inside. The space was a giant warehouse, cool and dark, except for the glow from four giant lava lamps like the one they'd seen on the way in. No one greeted them, and Vanessa was surprised to find only about thirty people there. They sat cross-legged on the floor in little clusters, finger-painting on the pages of old encyclopedias and looking completely spaced out, like they hadn't slept since the party started back in March. No one was drinking anything or eating anything or even talking. It was sort of like an anti-party party.

Vanessa watched as a woman wearing a fuzzy red bathrobe and red rubber rain boots chopped off a handful of her long dark hair and dropped it into a huge pot sitting on a hotplate on the floor. A tall, pale, skinny guy wearing only a black fedora hat and black boxer shorts went up to the pot and stirred it with a wooden yardstick.

"Bruce," Beverly greeted the guy with a nod. "This is Vanessa. She makes films."

Bruce nodded and kept on nodding for longer than normal as he stirred the pot. Vanessa wished desperately that she had her video camera with her. She'd never seen anything quite like this.

"Are you here to make a donation?" Bruce asked.

Vanessa wasn't sure who he was talking to. In fact, for the first time in her life, she felt completely lost. Every party she'd ever been to had been predictable to the point of being hopelessly boring. She smiled tentatively at Beverly. It was sort of nice to be surprised.

The music suddenly shifted to the soundtrack for *Shrek 2* and Vanessa felt more lost than ever. She took a step forward and peered into Bruce's pot. "What is that anyway?"

Bruce held up his left hand and wiggled his fingers. The top joint on the middle finger of his left hand was missing, just like Beverly's.

"I'm working on a regeneration project," Bruce said, as if that explained everything.

Beverly held up his left hand and spread his fingers out like a fan. No, Vanessa wasn't insane. His middle finger really *was* missing its top. "Most of us have contributed. But there's no pressure or anything."

Well, isn't that a relief?

Vanessa wasn't easily creeped out, but she was getting close. "And what do you do with the . . . parts and stuff . . . in the pot . . . after they're like, cooked or whatever?"

Bruce grinned and blue veins stood out on his pale neck. He looked like he hadn't eaten in months. "It's not about the doing; it's about the stirring," he responded.

Beverly nodded in that same odd, prolonged way that Bruce had nodded before. "Vanessa's got a great space," he volunteered, apropos of nothing. "I'm thinking of crashing there for a while. It'd be great for something like this," he added, still nodding.

All of a sudden Vanessa realized that looking for roommates on the Internet probably wasn't such a great idea.

Beverly had seemed interesting at first, but she'd almost rather live with Dan, despite all his failings, or one of her spoiled, vain, fashion-obsessed classmates than come home to a pot of boiling fingers and who knew what else on her stove. It was one thing to make art that people *thought* was shocking and bizarre without actually *trying* to be shocking and bizarre. Beverly and his friends were in college—hadn't they learned *anything*?

"Are you thirsty?" Beverly asked her. "Do you want some water?"

Vanessa realized that was just about the nicest thing he'd said to her all night. She couldn't believe she'd been worried about the configuration of her moles, or that she'd actually worn perfume just for him. She yawned and glanced around the enormous space. "I'm not sure how much more of this I can take," she responded, mimicking what Beverly had said about Dan's singing in the club. "I'm going home."

Beverly bit his lip. "But this is working. I mean—so far, right?" he asked.

"Actually, it's not." Vanessa imitated the sweet, fake smile her classmate Blair Waldorf flashed, telepathically telling the teacher to eat shit and die when she was trying to get excused from class early to attend a Manolo Blahnik sale.

"Sure you don't want to make a donation?" Bruce asked, still stirring the pot.

Vanessa unclipped her lip ring and tossed it in. "Good luck with that," she told them, turning to go.

Beverly and Bruce began to nod.

And as far as we know, they're still nodding.

what girls really do behind closed hotel suite doors

"Remember when we were in fifth grade and we used to practice kissing with pillows?" Serena buried her face in one of the Plaza's fluffy king-sized goose-down pillows and began making out with it. "Oh, *baby*," she cooed. "Your lips are so amazing."

Blair chucked a pillow at the back of Serena's head. "Have you been listening to me?" she demanded. "I said I almost kissed Stanford Parris the Fifth!"

Serena turned her head to one side and blew her hair out of her face. She'd taken off her skirt, and her white cotton underwear sagged halfway down her skinny ass. "So why didn't you?"

"I don't know." Blair untied the gold Cartier Yale pendant from around her neck and threw it on the bedside table. Then she yanked her dress off over her head, stripping down to her underwear. She pulled on one of the Plaza's white terry robes and cracked open a can of Coke. "I wanted to, but I couldn't stop laughing. And then I felt stupid, so I left."

Serena rolled over and started poking her nonexistent stomach fat. "Don't you think it's weird that we're friends and we're attracted to such different guys? I mean, I thought he was totally stuck-up."

Attracted to such different guys? Is that why they both lost their virginity to the *same* guy? Not that either of them wanted to wreck their friendship *again* by bringing *that* up.

Blair burped noisily. "You think everyone's stuck-up. And actually I think he was sort of embarrassed about being into Yale after I told him I was wait-listed. He's only, like, a C student at Andover. He doesn't even take any APs. The only reason he got in was because of his grandfather."

Serena's eyes opened wide. She was a B+ student and didn't take any APs either, but she'd gotten in. And while talking to Mr. Parris she'd basically decided once and for all that Yale was the school for her. Did she dare tell Blair and ruin a perfectly good time together in their own hotel suite?

Blair burped again and Serena thumped her frosted pink polished toes against the mattress, thinking. *Nah,* she decided. Besides, she suspected that the only reason Blair was so hung up on Stan 5 was because she thought he might help her get into Yale.

That's the problem with best friends. Sometimes they know you better than you know yourself.

"Hey, let's make prank calls!" Serena cried, desperate to change the subject. She sat up and grabbed the phone, stabbing giddily at the keypad.

"Hello? Concierge? Could you send a plumber to room 448? There's a terrible . . . er . . . *problem* with the toilet. Get what I'm saying? Great. Thank you." She dialed another number. "Sir? Is this room 448? Yes, this is the concierge. I just wanted to let you know that the male escort you ordered is on his way up." Then she dialed one of the suites down the hall. "Daddy, I can't sleep," she said in a baby voice. "Sing me a song." The guy on the other end started singing the Raves song "Ice Cream." He sounded exactly like Damian.

Hmm, wonder why?

"Wow, you're really good," Serena breathed in her baby voice. "I love you, Daddy," she cooed, and then hung up. She turned to Blair. "Okay, that was dumb."

Blair didn't say anything. She still couldn't believe she'd chickened out with Stan 5. It was only a kiss, and it wasn't like Nate even cared who she kissed, because he seemed to have totally forgotten about her.

All of a sudden there was a knock at the door.

"Shit!" Serena squealed, diving under the covers. "It's the concierge!"

Blair tightened the belt on her bathrobe and padded over to the door. "Who is it?" she called out, touching the door with nervous fingertips.

"It's me," Nate's voice answered.

Blair jumped backwards as if she'd been electrocuted. She tugged on the belt of her bathrobe again. "Who?" she demanded irritably, even though she knew perfectly well who it was.

"It's me, Nate," he called through the closed door. "Can I come in?"

"Psst!" Serena whispered from the bed. "Pretend I'm Stan 5!"

Blair turned around to find Serena sprawled facedown on the bed under the duvet, her long legs spread wide, her hair hidden discreetly under a pillow, and her rather large feet sticking out at the end of the bed. She totally passed for a guy. Even the rumpled little gray skirt on the floor could easily have been a pair of boxers.

Serena lifted her head and grinned devilishly. Blair giggled and waved her back into place. Then she opened the door, but only about four inches. "Now's not really a good time," she whispered mysteriously.

Nate looked disheveled and tired. In fact, she was pretty sure he was wearing exactly the same faded black T-shirt and khakis that he'd been wearing when she'd left his house the afternoon before, and his hair was definitely dirty, because there were no gold highlights in it. It just looked brown. Also, there was dark brown crap between his teeth, like brownie crumbs.

Or pre-chewed Oreos.

"I need to take a shower," Nate yawned.

"Well, you can't do it here." Blair insisted. She readjusted her bathrobe to insinuate that she was naked underneath. Then she took a step backward so Nate could see into the room. "I'm busy."

She watched as Nate's gaze traveled from the gold-and-white-painted door across the golden beige carpet to the bed. Two nights ago she would have grabbed him by the scruff of the neck and hurled him on top of the covers so she could ravage his ridiculously hot body and he could ravage hers, just like they'd been doing since she decided to go all the way. But he hadn't called her in two whole days and he really needed to brush his teeth. He'd missed his chance.

From beneath the covers, Serena did her best imitation of a studly postsex snore. Blair clenched her teeth to keep from smiling. Actually she didn't much feel like smiling. She was too pissed off at Nate.

Nate pressed his palms against his cheeks like he was trying to hold his face together. He'd been counting on staying with Blair tonight a) because she was in a hotel suite and it would be awesome to take a nice hot shower, have lots of sex, take a bubble bath, order tons of room service, and watch movies until they fell asleep in each other's arms; b) because he really didn't want to go home and endure the wrath of Admiral Archibald. He'd definitely be grounded, which meant he wouldn't be able to go out at all for the rest of his life, and he'd probably never see Blair again; and c) because while he was fooling around with Lexie he'd realized that he really didn't enjoy kissing anyone but Blair anymore.

Well, maybe he should have thought of that, like, yesterday.

Serena kicked her foot and bellowed through her nose like a sleeping elephant.

Who the fuck is that anyway? Nate was dying to ask, but the thought of knowing who it was made him press his hands against his face even harder. His gaze shifted back to Blair, who looked like she was already bored with whatever game they were playing.

"I was on the boat," he started to explain. "I lost my phone." Then he realized that didn't really explain anything.

Sometimes it just sucks to be you, doesn't it?

"Go home, Nate," Blair dismissed him. "Your parents are looking for you."

Nate let go of his face, stuffed his hands into his pockets and took a step backwards toward the elevators. Chocolate Oreo gunk was smeared on the crotch of his pants. He was a mess. "You haven't heard anything from Yale yet, have you?" he asked in a lame effort to find some common ground.

"No," she responded coldly.

Nate waited for her to say something more but she didn't. Instead, Blair stretched her arms over her head and yawned lazily, like she'd been having so much sex with the big, hot, studly man in her bed she couldn't even talk.

"Why don't you e-mail me or something?" she told Nate, and reached for the door handle.

As if she and Nate had ever communicated by e-mail.

When you saw someone naked every day for hours after school, it was hardly necessary to e-mail them.

The corners of Nate's mouth drooped like he was about to cry. Blair wasn't breaking up with him officially—she never did, which was why they'd been breaking up and getting back together on and off for the last three years. But that was before they'd become as intimate as you can be with someone, and now there was some random guy in Blair's bed. "Okay. Have a good day at school tomorrow."

"See you," Blair closed the door and leaned against it. "He's gone," she whispered.

Serena lifted her head and her pale blond hair cascaded all over the bed. "That was fun," she observed, but the way she said it made it sound like a question.

Blair went over and sat down on the end of the bed. "Really fun," she agreed hollowly. The girls' eyes met. Neither of them was smiling.

Then Serena giggled. "I guess it would have been more fun if I'd *really* been Stan 5."

Blair didn't say anything. She'd basically just broken up with Nate—again—after passing up a perfectly good opportunity to fool around with a boy who could very well get her into Yale. Well, one thing was for sure: She wasn't about to let Stan 5 get away.

Serena threw back the covers and grabbed the leather-bound room service menu from the bedside table. "Let's order filet mignons and French fries and beer and watch old movies!"

She'd always been an expert at changing the subject.

Blair scooted her feet up underneath her and reached for the TV remote. There might be an Audrey Hepburn movie on TCM or AMC. She flicked through the channels hopefully. Aha! *My Fair Lady*. Well, at least that was something.

Serena lit a Merit Ultra Light, took a puff, and then stuck it in Blair's mouth. Then she picked up the phone, massaging Blair's shoulders as she ordered nearly everything on the Plaza Hotel's room service menu.

Maybe life sucked for some people, but Serena wouldn't allow it to suck for them.

two doors down, a suite gets trashed

Just down the hall, in an even bigger suite, Dan, Jenny, two members of the Raves, and a very tan French girl were lounging around smoking cigars that had been FedExed to the room from Cuba that day. The whole room was filled with ripped-open FedEx boxes: peaches from Georgia, candles from France, vodka from Finland, strong brown ale from Ireland, breadsticks from Italy, shower gel from LA, and extra-sharp cheddar cheese from Vermont.

As if you couldn't buy all of the above in the city that has *everything*.

Lloyd asked the concierge to send up more bathrobes, and one by one they all removed their clothes and donned robes. Jenny wasn't quite sure what to do with her pants and shirt, and it was nearly impossible to hide her bra, because the bathrobe had the troublesome habit of popping outward in the cleavage area. She decided to stuff her clothes into the gold-and-white vanity cupboard under the bathroom sink and cinched the belt of the bathrobe as tight as it would go before stepping out into the suite once more.

"Have a peach," Damian offered in his adorable Irish accent. He pulled one of the perfectly ripened fruits out of the box and held it up. He'd changed into a robe, and Jenny wondered if he was still wearing his underwear. The thought made her cheeks turn red and her bathrobe pop open once more. Damian patted the seat cushion of the gold damask loveseat he was sitting on. "Come, sit down. Eat one of these and then show me how badly you can kick my ass at Terminator."

Jenny glanced at the selection of PlayStation games on the coffee table. Kick his ass? She'd never played a video game in her life.

"Or would you prefer something more refined, like a fine Italian breadstick?" Lloyd asked from the sofa on the other side of the coffee table. He drummed two breadsticks on his knees. "They're excellent with ale. Just dunk," he explained, dipping an entire breadstick into a bottle of Irish ale, "and munch." Then he patted the seat cushion next to him just like Damian had done. "Try it."

Unable to decide which guy was cuter, Jenny sliced a tiny piece of cheddar cheese off the huge brick of it on the coffee table and then knelt down on the floor. Monique was sitting on the floor too, smoking a hand-rolled cigarette and reading a French fashion magazine and looking bored because Dan had gone into the bathroom to shower and change into his robe.

"Ooh la la, I just realized who you are!" Monique squealed, ashing on the floor in her excitement. "You're zee model in zee fantastique *W* pages. I love zohze photos. And zat blond girl— so beautiful, *non?*"

"Well, you're even prettier," Jenny responded shyly, thrilled to be recognized. She wished she had a cool French accent like Monique's. Everything sounded so much cooler with an accent.

Dan came out of the bathroom with his hip-hop clothes all wadded up under his arm. Now that he was de-puked and had sobered up a little, he was tempted to chuck the clothes out the window.

"Hey man, you never told us your sister was a bloody fashion model," Damian said.

"If bloody Monique is impressed, she must be pretty fucking huge," Lloyd agreed.

Boys. Give them some strong Irish ale and all of a sudden they all have British accents.

Dan was so ashamed of his performance that night, he could barely look at his bandmates. "She's done some modeling," he mumbled.

Marc, the Raves' bassist, opened the door of the suite, back from a walk with his Bernese mountain dog, Trish. Trish was huge and black with a sweet brown-and-white face like a St. Bernard. He'd named the dog after his ex-girlfriend—the love of his life, who'd broken up with him back in ninth grade—and he never went anywhere without her.

How sweet. And how creepy.

Dan sat on the floor next to his sister. Trish lay down next to him and put her head in his lap. She had terrible breath, like she'd been eating canned mackerel and spoiled milk.

"Hey Marc. Turns out Jenny is, like, this hugely famous supermodel," Lloyd announced.

Marc glanced shyly at Jenny, then picked up one of the Plaza Hotel bathrobes from the stack and put it on over his clothes. He looked like a modern-day vampire, with curly black hair, pale skin, and nearly black eyes.

Jenny giggled, reveling in all the attention. It was one o'clock in the morning and she was at the Plaza Hotel, wearing only a bathrobe and underwear, with the members of the coolest band ever! It was kind of weird being there with her brother, but kind of reassuring, too.

Monique sat up on her knees and stroked Trish's ears. Then she slipped her hand down the back of Dan's bathrobe. "Come into zee bedroom," she mouthed against his ear.

Jenny could hear every word Monique said—not that she really wanted to. Boldly, she stood up and went over to the sofa to sit next to Lloyd. After all, she was a famous model—she could sit wherever she liked.

Lloyd handed her a breadstick. "In southern Italy these are considered an aphrodisiac."

"Liar!" Damian threw a ripe, juicy peach at Lloyd's head. It missed and splattered all over the pristine white wall behind him.

You're not a real rock star unless you know how to trash a hotel room.

"Don't listen to that butthead, he's full of it," Damian warned, suddenly losing his Irish accent. He dragged three PlayStation joysticks over to the sofa and sat down, so that Jenny was wedged between him and Lloyd.

As if she minded.

Jenny's feet were tingling and her ears were buzzing. It was a school night and she was a supermodel hanging out in a hotel room with three famous rock stars. If only Serena could see her now.

Monique dragged Dan into a standing position. Damian's foot flew up and kicked her in the butt, but Monique pretended not to notice. She pulled Dan into the adjacent bedroom, slamming the door behind them.

"Don't make too much noise!" Damian shouted after them.

Marc lay down where Dan and Monique had been sitting

and rested his head on his dog. Trish licked his pale cheek and wrapped an enormous black paw around his neck.

Aw. What a cute couple.

Jenny had never felt so famous in her life, and she owed it all to her brother. He deserved to hook up with some random French girl. And she deserved to be wedged between the two cutest guys ever to grace the cover of *Rolling Stone*. If only some reporter would knock on the door and take their picture. She kind of wanted the world to find out about this—it was too good not to be known, even if she got into major trouble.

No worries, darling—the world has a funny way of finding out nearly *everything*.

 gossipgirl.co.uk

hey people!

And you thought the Tribeca Star was so cool

The Plaza Hotel is having a revival, a *big* one. Some of our favorite people were suite-wrecking at the Plaza last night. It happened too late to make it into today's papers, but log onto the *New York Post*'s Page Six online, and it's all there. A whole black-and-white photo-montage of adorable little **J** getting kissed good-bye *on the lips* by the lead guitarist of the Raves right on the Plaza's red-carpeted steps and getting spanked on her bottom by the drummer with his drumsticks before he swept her into a bear hug. She even wore her Plaza Hotel bathrobe home, carelessly leaving her clothes behind, and blew kisses from the taxi, like a modern-day Marilyn Monroe.

J wasn't the only budding model to hook up with the Raves' lead guitarist. A hotel staff member actually recorded him singing to **S** over a Plaza house phone. **S** finished the phone call saying, "I love you, Daddy." Oh does she?

But what about his marriage to a mysterious French girl a year or so back, in an exclusive ceremony in St. Barts? If you study the photograph of him kissing **J**, he *is* wearing a gold band on the ring finger of his left hand . . . and there *was* a beautiful French girl on the scene as well, although she was totally preoccupied with **D**, the band's raging new front man. His debut public performance was actually kind of embarrassing, but, like a typical French girl, she's probably too horny to care.

The confusing part is that **S** was staying with **B** in *her* suite, bringing to mind those old stories about **S** and **B** in a hot tub together, engaging in what is best described as a little girl-on-girl. As if things weren't juicy and complicated enough already!!

There's something about those French girls

I know I've ranted about this before, but why is it that the girls who go to L'École Française look twenty-five when they're only fourteen? And how come all the guys we know secretly or not so secretly lust after them? And how positively infuriating to hear a group of L'École girls talking about you at a party—in Franglish, so that you can hardly understand a word they're saying. They eat only hot chocolate and pommes frites, they chain smoke, and you never see them jogging or playing field hockey in Central Park. Yet none of them are fat or zit-ridden. It's as thought their mères and grandmères introduced them to Lancôme and Chanel when they were only babes, and the alpha hydroxy acids or whatever permeated their systems, leaving them with perfect skin, perfect bodies, and feet that are most comfortable in three-inch heels. Their school even *allows* heels—unlike all the other girls' schools on the Upper East Side— which basically proves my point. When it comes to educating girls, the French seem to follow a completely different curriculum. Not that we're jealous or anything.

Other sightings

B's mom at the Italian Consulate waving her checkbook around— what exactly is she up to now? **K** and **I** getting matching bikini waxes at Maria Bonita, a tiny NoLita salon, conveniently located near Sigerson Morrison, which happened to be having a sale. **C** (who dropped off the radar for a while there after getting rejected at every college he applied to) taking his white monkey to be er . . . fixed . . . at a discreet Chelsea clinic. It seems the monkey had inherited its owner's penchant for flirtation and has been throwing itself at every dog, cat, and ferret in the neighborhood.

Your e-mail

 Dear GG,
I know it was you who made the film everyone's so excited

about at Cannes. What are you waiting for? Get your ass over here and collect your reward!
—mogl

A: Dear mogl,
You might think the lady doth protest too much, but I'm saying this for the last time: I have no f—ing clue what you're talking about! Enjoy Cannes.
—GG

Q: Dear GG,
What are we supposed to do the rest of the year now that we know where we're going to college?
—bord

A: Dear bord,
Please—isn't this what we've all been waiting for? Time to shop, drink, eat, and be merry? Time to be all we can be? If you don't have your own pool and can't get into the SoHo House rooftop pool, make it your mission to befriend someone with pool access and spend the rest of May rotating Eres bikinis!
—GG

Q: Dear GG,
If you really really like a girl but she keeps ignoring you, what should you do?
—2bummed

A: Dear 2bummed,
First, change your screen name to something more upbeat and attractive like "superhot." Second, make sure your deodorant works and that your outfit isn't completely hopeless. Then ask her to hang out, preferably where there are other people she knows and feels comfortable with, so she can have fun even if she decides you're a self-effacing loser and she's not interested. Good luck!
—GG

It's Monday, the start of the school week—I know: *yawn*. Realistically, though, after a weekend like this, how boring can things be? Like wolves in sheep's clothing, we all look so innocent in our school uniforms, but this weekend won't go without repercussions.

I'll be the first to report when the shit hits!

You know you love me,

gossip girl

j, b, and *s* are totally getting expelled

"I heard that freshman slut had, like, group sex with every member of the band—even the new lead singer, who's like, her *brother*," Kati Farkas whispered to her best friend and Constance Billard School Senior Spa Weekend co-planner, Isabel Coates. Kati reparted her long, strawberry blond hair with a pink tortoiseshell comb, smoothing it down with her hands. "Did you see those pictures of her in the *Post* online? She didn't even bother to get dressed before she left the hotel!"

The two girls were peering out the third-floor windows of the Constance Billard School library, pretending to memorize their lines for the girls-in-bikinis-and-mud-masks skit they were supposed to put on in the senior lounge tomorrow to promote Senior Spa Weekend. Not that it needed promoting. Everyone would take home gift bags full of fabulous new Origins products, and their skin would absolutely glow until graduation. It was going to be the coolest Senior Cut Day ever.

Isabel grabbed the comb out of Kati's hands and combed her sleek dark hair back into a ponytail. "I heard Nate and his friends almost died in a shipwreck, but Blair was too busy hooking up with Serena *again* to even notice. Can you imagine finding out your girlfriend was cheating on you with, like, another *girl?*"

Kati made a face and shuddered in agreement. "Gross."

Isabel pressed her pug nose up against the window. "Look!"

Blair and Serena were walking hastily down Ninety-third Street, their arms linked, grinning slyly like they'd just shared the most entertaining secret. Instead of the usual socially acceptable midthigh length, Blair's uniform hung all the way down to her knees. It was totally obvious that she'd borrowed the uniform from Serena.

Nudge, nudge.

Just as the girls were turning into the great blue doors of the Constance Billard School, a yellow taxi pulled up, and Jenny Humphrey stepped out, munching on a breadstick. She'd managed to change out of her Plaza Hotel bathrobe and into a pink T-shirt and her blue-and-white-seersucker Constance Billard spring uniform. She was also wearing a pair of rather fetching hot pink Jimmy Choo platform sandals that were totally out of uniform, and an enormous pair of pink tortoiseshell Jackie O. sunglasses.

Uh-oh, don't look now, but someone thinks she's *hot stuff*.

"Where did she get those shoes?" Kati breathed in disbelief. "The waiting list for those is like a mile long."

"They're probably fakes; you just can't tell from here," Isabel replied.

Neither girl wanted to admit what they were really thinking—that Damian or Lloyd from the Raves had probably given Jenny the shoes and the glasses—because to be jealous of a freshman was so completely uncool.

Serena, Blair, and Jenny had only just stepped inside the doors when they were accosted by Mrs. M, Constance Billard's formidable headmistress.

"Girls," Mrs. M commanded. "I'd like to talk to all three of you in my office, please. Your parents are on their way."

Huh? All three girls wondered in unison.

This should be fun.

Mrs. M's face was doughy and soft, and her hair was dyed Raggedy Ann auburn and permed into little ringlets, giving her a sweet, grandmotherly appearance. But appearances lie: she was anything but sweet. In fact, she was a big, mean old dyke who purportedly kept a tractor-driving girlfriend in her house upstate and had a tattoo on her thigh that said, "Ride Me, Vonda."

"Sit down, girls," she ordered, arranging her wide, navy blue Talbots pantsuit–clad ass on the period chair behind her giant mahogany desk. Mrs. M's office was decorated entirely in red, white, and blue, and the Constance girls weren't quite sure if she actually thought she was the president or if she was just extremely patriotic.

In a daze of obedience, Serena, Blair, and Jenny planted themselves on the stiff blue loveseat opposite Mrs. M's desk. The loveseat was a little crowded with all three of them on it, but the nearness was comforting.

"Two of you are meant to be graduating next month, after which you are no longer my responsibility," Mrs. M began. "One of you, however, has only just begun her high-school career, and you're already headed in a very bad direction, no thanks to the two of you seniors." She propped a pair of half-glasses on her nose and sorted through a bunch of files on her desk. "All three of you are in a very precarious position."

Blair opened her mouth to speak, but then closed it again when her mother appeared in the doorway of Mrs. M's office, dressed in tennis whites and carrying a fussing and whimpering Yale in a Burberry baby sling. The sling hadn't been adjusted properly and it banged against her hip like a cumbersome tote bag.

"I'm trying this new thing called 'attachment parenting,'" Eleanor explained breathlessly. "It's supposed to make your children bond with you and increase their confidence." She giggled and hitched the sling up on her shoulder awkwardly. "I think you're supposed to walk around like this all day long, but who has the time? I've got tennis at the Y, lunch at Daniel, and a facial at Arden, and Cyrus and I are going out to Bridgehampton later this week. Half an hour on Mondays and Wednesdays is all the bonding time I have!"

Still, she gets points for trying.

"Oh, and Blair, dear, there's a Dior sample sale I thought you might be interested in going to. It's at noon. You could meet me there."

Mrs. M raised an unplucked brown eyebrow. Shopping during school hours—heaven forbid! Although if it had been a Talbots sample sale, even she might have been tempted.

"Mrs. Rose." Mrs. M pointed efficiently to the wing-backed chair next to the loveseat upon which the girls were perched. "I realize you're busy, but I wanted to express my concern about the fact that your daughter is apparently living in a hotel. With her acceptance at Yale University hanging in the balance, I hardly think it's appropriate for a young woman to be living in such . . ." She paused, searching for the appropriate words. "An undisciplined environment."

Eleanor beamed cluelessly back at the headmistress. She had noticed that Blair had gone away for the weekend, but she wasn't exactly sure where, and she hadn't really noticed that Blair hadn't come home last night, because she and Cyrus had gone to a cocktail party to celebrate the opening of one of his new buildings and hadn't come home until nearly two themselves. She sat down in an armchair to the left of Mrs. M's desk and crossed her legs, tucking Yale up under her arm like the latest Hermès Birkin bag. Yale whined in protest, but Eleanor kept on smiling, as if she wasn't sure what else to do.

Blair squirmed uncomfortably in her place on the loveseat. With a mother like that, couldn't Mrs. M understand why she had to live in a hotel?

"Blair stayed over at my house last night," Serena fibbed. For someone who looked like Upper East Side Barbie, Serena was extremely good at thinking on her feet, or her Manolos, or whatever shoe-of-the-moment she happened to be wearing. "Look, she even borrowed one of my uniforms."

"Then why have I been fielding calls all morning from parents and prospective parents worried about their daughters sleeping in hotel rooms with drunken rock stars?" Mrs. M demanded. "I even had a publishing house call to inform me that next year Constance Billard will have the honor of being listed in their college guidebook as one of the five best schools to send your daughter to if you want her to be a celebrity or just date one."

"Cool," Jenny blurted out, and then immediately wished she hadn't.

Mrs. M shot her a don't-even-start-you-little-chickenshit glare. The headmistress seemed to be at a loss for giving Eleanor advice on how to raise her daughter, which must have been a frequent problem, considering the fact that most of the parents of the girls at Constance Billard didn't raise their daughters themselves. They had help, and lots of it.

"I'm sure if the girls were together they couldn't have done much harm," Eleanor commented with more savvy than Blair had thought she was capable of.

"We didn't even leave the room," Blair added, and then

clamped her mouth shut again. What was her problem anyway? Serena had just said they'd stayed at her house last night.

Then Serena's mother, Lillian van der Woodsen, and Jenny's father, Rufus Humphrey, suddenly appeared in the doorway of Mrs. M's office. Rufus was unaccustomed to leaving the house or even waking up before eleven o'clock and looked even more disheveled and outrageous than usual. His long, wiry salt-and-pepper hair was pulled into a bun updo and fastened with the huge glittery purple plastic hairclip Jenny had bought in fourth grade, and he was wearing gray sweatpants that had been cut off to a sort of midcalf clam-digger length and a red flannel shirt with one sleeve rolled up and a pack of unfiltered Camels sticking out of the breast pocket. His shoes were okay—vintage brown penny loafers—only not so good with the sweatpants and seriously awful without socks.

Mrs. van der Woodsen was her usual immaculately dressed and poised self, seeming to emanate an odor of fresh-cut lilies and French-milled soap. She hugged her long, tanned arms against her chest, risking wrinkling her mint green linen Chanel dress so that none of her body parts would get too close to Rufus.

"Sorry we're late for the inquisition," Rufus growled. He shot Jenny a threatening look. "I wouldn't have missed it for the world."

Mrs. van der Woodsen went over and graciously kissed Mrs. M on the cheek. It was the sort of kiss benefactors are used to bestowing on the directors of the organizations they so generously give millions of dollars to. "It's my fault the girls were late for school," she admitted. "My driver had to rush off to pick up my dry cleaning, so they were forced to walk."

Serena shot her mother a grateful glance and her mother blinked with silent understanding.

Now we know where Serena got her grace under pressure.

Baby Yale suddenly made the type of gastrointestinal noise that only babies are allowed to make in public. Eleanor whipped out her cell phone and dialed the nanny. She'd had quite enough bonding, thank you very much. She wasn't about to risk having to change a diaper. "Stay in the car, I'll be right out," she directed frantically.

Mrs. M looked like she'd suddenly realized there were way too many people in the room and that if she didn't do something about it, things were going to get extremely weird.

As if they weren't weird enough already.

The headmistress sighed heavily, as though her weekend up in Woodstock baling hay with Vonda had come and gone way too quickly, and maybe she'd better start thinking about early retirement. "Serena and Blair. You're seniors, your parents are busy people. Let's just leave it at this: You may be nearing adulthood, but I'd prefer it if you slept in your own beds, particularly on school nights."

Eleanor nodded and hastily gathered the howling Yale up in her sling as best she could, clearly eager to get the child safely into her nanny's capable hands. Mrs. van der Woodsen smiled ruefully, as if she were confident that any trouble Serena caused could be easily ironed out with a democratic kiss on the cheek and the promise of a large donation to Constance Billard's development fund. And Rufus grunted, like he couldn't wait to be alone in the room with Jenny and Mrs. M so he could give them both a piece of his mind.

The bell rang, signaling the end of first period.

"May we go to class now?" Blair asked sweetly, as if missing gym was *really* going to mess up her day.

"You may," Mrs. M relented. Serena and Blair stood up, leaving Jenny alone on the loveseat. "Just remember, girls," the headmistress added, "your acceptance at college can be revoked if you do not maintain the standards promised on your record."

"Thank you for the warning," Serena replied, bobbing her head in a sort of obedient half-curtsy before grabbing Blair's elbow and booking out of the room. They kissed their mothers good-bye and then took the stairs up to the senior lounge three at a time, breathlessly repeating over and over, *"What the hell was that?!"*

"Jennifer," Mrs. M and Rufus said, practically in unison.

Jenny crossed her ankles and sat on her hands, feeling very small and unprotected now that the two older girls had gone. Her father sat down beside her on the loveseat and put his arm around her shoulders. He smelled like stale onion bagels and bad coffee. There were little cigarette burns all over his sweatpants.

"You've always been a pretty good kid." He gave Jenny's shoulders a squeeze. "Good grades. Great artist. Reads a lot. Nice to her daddy—most of the time." He shot Mrs. M an amused look. "Are you going to tell me I've been deluded all these years?"

Mrs. M smiled her first genuine smile in weeks. She liked Rufus Humphrey. Sure, he was scruffy and inappropriate, but he was a single dad who'd raised two kids himself and done a decent job of it. His only trouble was that he lived on the other side of the park and didn't play by the same rules that the rest of the Upper East Side had played by since they started nursery school at Brick Church on Park Avenue. He'd never given a cent to the school's endowment or attended a fundraiser. He'd never offered to build the school a new library or gym or swimming pool if it could guarantee Jenny a place at Harvard after graduation. He was also more protective of his daughter than most of the parents she was used to, mainly because he'd changed her diapers himself, and stayed up with her when she couldn't sleep, and punished her when she'd done wrong, and therefore felt a certain personal responsibility for how she behaved.

Whoa, what a concept.

Jenny seriously hoped that this was one of the weird dreams she often had when she ate too many Entenmann's chocolate donuts. Not that she'd eaten any donuts recently. As far as she could remember, all she'd eaten for dinner last night were six fine breadsticks imported from Italy via Federal Express to a particular suite at the Plaza Hotel.

Not to mention the seventh, which she'd wrapped in a gold-embroidered Plaza Hotel hand towel as a memento.

"Thank you for coming at such short notice, Mr. Humphrey," Mrs. M began. "And I have to admit I agree. Jennifer is an intelligent, creative, and mostly well-behaved girl. However, she is building a reputation, for being . . . a little wild, and the parents of her peers are beginning to ask questions."

Rufus gave his beard a perplexed tug. As a self-proclaimed anarchist he must have felt supremely uncomfortable in Mrs. M's patriotically decorated office, having to defer to an authority figure about his daughter's supposed wild behavior.

"What do you mean by 'a reputation for being a little wild?'"

Mrs. M took off her glasses and folded them carefully in front of her. "Mr. Humphrey, are you aware that your daughter was not at home last night?"

Rufus nodded. "You got a problem with that?"

Jenny giggled and then clamped her hand over her mouth.

"Well, where do you imagine that she was?" Mrs. M persisted, her soft, rag-doll face becoming more and more stern by the minute.

Rufus snorted, and Jenny could sense his anarchist blood beginning to boil. "I don't have to *imagine* where she was. She *told* me. She spent the night at her friend Elise's house. Right around here somewhere."

"Elise Wells," Jenny elaborated hoarsely. "She's in my class."

"Yes. Well. Elise wasn't an hour late to school this morning. In fact, she arrived at school on time and alone. Your daughter, however, only just arrived. And that is because she had to go home and change first. Because, in fact, she spent the night at a hotel, in a suite, with a rather well known rock music group."

Rufus's jaw fell open, revealing his crooked, coffee-stained teeth. For once, he was completely speechless. Jenny hugged her arms against her chest, keeping her eyes fixed on the royal blue rug.

"This isn't her first mishap, either," Mrs. M continued. "There was that compromising image of her and a boy that was passed around the Internet a few months back. Afterwards, I sent you a letter suggesting Jennifer see a therapist a few times a week here at school, to which you never responded. And then last month Jennifer appeared in a popular teen magazine in only an exercise bra, upsetting more than a few of her classmates' parents—mostly those who also have teenage sons."

Rufus swiped his hand over his face. "Jesus, Jenny," he breathed.

Even Jenny had to agree that Mrs. M made her sound like

a first-class slut, but she wasn't even going to try to defend herself. Besides, she'd been mostly good most of her life—it was kind of exciting being the bad girl.

"So are you suspending her, or what?" her dad demanded.

Yes, please. Jenny thought with silent pleasure. *And send me straight to boarding school.*

Mrs. M shook her head. "Not yet. This is only a warning. But if Jennifer continues to behave in such a publicly flagrant way, or in a way that upsets her schoolmates and their parents, I will have to take measures to ensure that the reputation of this institution remains intact."

The third bell rang, signaling the start of second period.

"I'm missing Latin," Jenny squeaked. "May I go?"

"Not so fast, missy," her father bellowed, tightening his grip around her shoulders. Rufus was a softy at heart, but he did a mean disciplinarian act when he was pissed off.

"That's all right. You are both dismissed," Mrs. M responded. She pushed her chair back and folded her arms across her chest, looking dykier than ever.

Jenny jumped to her feet and hurried out of the office before her father could catch up and have the last word—and before Mrs. M could send her home for being so completely out of uniform.

"You look tired, Mr. Humphrey," she heard Mrs. M say behind her. "I've got a wonderful farm in Woodstock. You really should visit sometime."

"Woodstock—I love Woodstock!" Rufus exclaimed. "I camped out there back in 1974. I was living in a van with a couple of poet pals—"

Jenny bolted upstairs to Latin, oddly thrilled at how close she'd come to getting expelled from Constance. Who cared if her picture was in the gossip columns as an unidentified, short, curly-haired, "publicly flagrant" floozy? Eventually she'd be recognized as the girl who always hung out with the Raves. People would constantly ask if *she* was Damian's girlfriend, and she'd be a Page Six girl, just like she'd always wanted!

n's personal little cluster*%@#

"A Pyrrhic victory," Mr. Knoeder mumbled in his typical impossible-to-follow manner. "Archibald. Are you with me?"

Nate hadn't done his homework. He wasn't even sure what day it was. He'd woken up, taken a shower, and wandered into school, hoping for some guidance. Now this asswipe of a history teacher wanted him to answer some idiotic question about the Vietnam War, which everyone knew had been a total clusterfuck.

"Pyrrhus was a Greek king or whatever who kicked the shit out of the Romans in some battle, but there were a ton of casualties," Nate heard himself saying. *No wonder I got into Yale* and *Brown,* he congratulated himself. *I'm a frigging genius!*

"Actually, it was the *Battle* of Pyrrhus," Mr. Knoeder corrected, sticking his pinky in his ear as he wrote something on the board. The St. Jude's boys all called him Mr. No Dick because he wore his pants so high and so tight, he couldn't possibly have had a dick. "But your answer was mostly accurate."

Nate got out his cell phone and started texting Jeremy, who was seated in the same row as he was, four desks down.

HEY THKS DICKLESS, he wrote.

WNT 2 HANG L8R? Jeremy wrote back.

CANT. GROUNDED, Nate replied.

SORRY 2 HEAR ABT B & THT KID, Jeremy wrote back.

Nate leaned over his desk and shot his friend an annoyed look that said, "Please explain."

KID FRM YALE PRTY THT HKEDUP W B, Jeremy clarified.

So that was who was in Blair's bed last night. Nate was too bummed to even reply. He'd left Blair alone for a little more than a day, and she'd had to go and hook up with some asshole at a stupid Yale party that she probably wasn't even invited to! He ought to have been furious. Instead, he just felt depressed. He was supposed to have been at that party. He could even have brought Blair with him. They could have talked about the future and then had sex afterwards. It might have been romantic. But as usual he'd messed everything up.

Well, now he knows—it may not suck to be the cheater, but it definitely sucks to be cheated on.

Fuck it, Nate decided. He held up his hand. "Mr. Knoeder, may I be excused? I think I have food poisoning or something."

Oh, come now. You can do better than that.

Mr. Knoeder didn't even notice. His back was turned as he busily drew a detailed map of Saigon in purple chalk. Nate texted a despondent SEE YA to Jeremy, gathered up his things, and slipped out of the classroom, leaving the rest of the St. Jude's senior U.S. history class to stare after him and wonder why they didn't have the balls to do the same.

Nate stuffed his books in his basement locker and slammed the door. Fuck homework, and fuck school. He was already into college, and now that he was grounded, he might as well just stay at home, eating brownies and getting high. He'd cut the rest of the day's classes, light up a big fatty, fill out the appropriate forms, and send in his deposit to Yale. So what that he'd promised Blair he wouldn't go to Yale unless she got in? Every promise they'd ever made to each other had been broken, and the truth was, Yale had the best lacrosse team and had promised to make him captain his sophomore year. He wanted to go there whether Blair got in or not.

With grim determination, he headed home, trying to rid himself of the image of that skinny, snoring, girlfriend-stealing asswipe sleeping in Blair's hotel bed. Mailing in his Yale deposit wasn't exactly going to be a victory without losses though. Blair was going to spit fire when she heard about it.

Unless she didn't care anymore, which was almost even scarier.

d, the future of hip-hop

Riverside Prep was housed in a redbrick church built in the late 1900s, the quaintest little schoolhouse on the Upper West Side. The school's main entrance was on West End Avenue—a cute bright red door over which hung a sign that said RIVERSIDE PREPARATORY SCHOOL FOR BOYS, which sounded embarrassingly like some sort of rich boys' finishing school. Thankfully, the upper-school boys entered from the side entrance, a normal-looking black door on Seventy-seventh Street, the perfect place to slip into school nearly two hours late.

Dan swaggered into the last ten minutes of first-period AP English wearing his hip-hop pants and black-and-yellow sneakers from the Raves gig the night before, and a dark gray APC T-shirt given to him by Monique with MR. WONDERFUL stenciled in bold red letters across the chest. Last night he'd drunk his ass off, sung like a sickass motherfucker, and then had crazy, totally undeserved sex with a beautiful French girl on a giant bed in a Plaza Hotel suite. Being a rock star was actually kind of excellent.

You don't say.

"Well, if it isn't my most famous student," Ms. Solomon observed tersely as Dan wandered to the back of the room and slouched behind a desk. Ms. Solomon was right out of graduate school and was incredibly ashamed of the major crush she had on Dan. Instead of showering him with praise—there was no question he was the most accomplished and intellectual student in the class—she was either snide and critical, or she ignored him completely. Once, just to test her, he'd even copied an essay on Virginia Woolf's writing habits, written by the famous literary critic Harold Bloom, her advisor at Princeton, and handed it in, pretending he'd written it. Ms. Solomon had given him a B+, just like she did on every one of his English assignments, no matter how bad or good it was.

"The class and I were just discussing whether or not we should have a final essay on our unit on Shakespeare's tragedies instead of a final exam. Any opinion, Dan?" She clamped a hand over her mouth and added sarcastically. "I do apologize—perhaps you have a stage name now?"

Dan frowned down at his desktop, where someone had etched the words *Bitch Face* with a green ballpoint pen. Normally he would have welcomed the chance to write a paper over taking an exam, but papers required research and outlining and hours of writing, whereas an exam required a single two-hour appearance.

That is, if you have no intention of studying for it, which he didn't.

Now that he was a rock star he'd be touring, shooting videos, signing albums, and fending off women and the paparazzi. Two hours out of one day for a stupid English exam was definitely preferable.

Ms. Solomon was the type of dried-apple skinny that made her look forty years older than she probably was, and her hair, which she kept pulled back in a low ponytail, was an ashy dark blond color that looked gray under the school's harsh fluorescent lights. She loved lace, and preferred cream-colored blouses with lace collars and ruffles at the sleeves, paired with black wool knee-length skirts, black stockings, and bizarrely high, skinny-heeled black pumps. Her skirts were always seriously tight, too, leading the boys to suspect that she probably thought she was the sexiest female alive.

Ew.

"Half the class wants a paper and half the class wants an exam. Yours is the swing vote," she explained.

Meaning that no matter what Dan said, half the class would hate him for it.

He cleared his throat. "I think an exam would be a better indicator of how much we've learned over the course of the year," he declared, sounding like a total schmo.

"Oh, would it now?" Chuck Bass sneered from two desks away. Riverside Prep's dress code was plain-colored khaki pants or cords, brown or black belt, white or pastel-colored button-down shirt, and brown or black loafers with dark-colored socks. Chuck Bass was wearing a black Prada jumpsuit, unzipped so his tanned, recently waxed chest was clearly visible, and creamy white leather Camper sandals that showed off his smooth, manicured feet. On the floor beneath his desk, Chuck's pet snow monkey, Sweetie, poked his fuzzy white head out of Chuck's orange-and-red leather Dooney & Bourke tote bag and bared his teeth.

Chuck hardly deserved to be in AP English. He could barely spell, had never read a book in its entirety, and thought Beowulf was a type of fur used for lining coats. But in an effort to get him into college, his parents had insisted he be placed in all the APs, which turned out to be a big fat mistake. Due to the fact that Chuck preferred to shop and attend fashion shows instead of going to school and doing his homework, he had gotten Ds in all his classes last semester, failed to get into *any* of the colleges he'd applied to, and was now bound for military school.

And was he bitter? Definitely.

"Hey Mr. Wonderful," Chuck hissed at Dan. "Don't look now, but your days as a Rave are over."

Huh?

Dan slouched in his chair and dug at the desk with his ballpoint pen. He was a rock star; he didn't have to take this shit. Someone's foot nudged the base of his spine. "You're out," whispered Bryce James, one of Chuck's bullish friends. "Unless your slut of a sister can get you back in."

Dan's hackles rose. What did Jenny have to do with it? As far as he knew, Jenny was only going along for the ride, just like she'd always done. After all, if your big brother was in a major band, wouldn't you want to hang out with him and his bandmates, too?

"I heard she wants to be a singer," Bryce elaborated. "So she slept with every one of them."

Dan whipped around and gave Bryce the finger simply because he was too hungover to think of anything intelligent to say. Jenny had left the suite by the time he and Monique had gotten up that morning, but what exactly had she been up to while he was getting busy last night? And how come everyone already seemed to know about it?

"An exam it is, then," Ms. Solomon announced. She scribbled something in a notepad and then stood up and approached Dan's desk. "I'm a bit of a Raves fan myself," she murmured, her cheeks slightly flushed. "And it's sort of killing me." She stopped in front of Dan, put her palms on his desk, and leaned toward him so that he could smell the everything bagel with scallion cream cheese she'd eaten for breakfast. "Is it true that Damian is married to his high-school sweetheart? Some French girl?" she asked loudly, obviously thinking it was totally hip for a teacher to know anything about a cool band like the Raves.

Dan's hands were sweating, and he fingered the pack of unfiltered Camels in the back pocket of his baggy pants. Didn't Riverside Prep have rules about teachers harassing the students?

There were only two minutes left before the end of class. Still hoping to hear the answer to Ms. Solomon's question, the other boys quietly gathered their books and zipped up their backpacks.

The minute hand on the clock over the blackboard crept forward and the hallway outside the classroom buzzed to life. Dan stood up, brushed past his nosy teacher, and headed for the door.

Saved by the bell.

an e-mail worth responding to

That afternoon during computer lab, Serena was tempted to e-mail that melodramatic artist at Brown, those perky sorority weirdos at Princeton, and that lovelorn jock at Harvard, telling them to have nice lives, because from now on she was all about Yale. Instead, she permanently expunged them from her trash folder. At lunchtime she'd actually mailed in her deposit to Yale, and what a relief it was to have finally come to a decision—even if she couldn't tell her best friend in the whole world about it. She skimmed the rest of her e-mail until she came to one from an unknown source.

From: dpolk@raver.net
To: Svdwoodsen@constancebillard.edu
Subject: don't believe everything you read

So, we're an item. It's all very flattering. Problem is, we've never met. Want to? A bunch of people will be at my place in the Village Friday night. Hope you can make it.
Damian

Serena giggled and stood up partway out of her chair, searching the Constance Billard computer lab for Blair's dark shiny head. But Blair was working intently at her computer and didn't even notice Serena waving at her. Mr. Schneider, the uptight computer proctor with the deformed nostrils, glared at her, and Serena went back to her e-mail. She knew from their videos that the Raves' lead guitarist was extremely handsome and talented, and wouldn't it be crazy if they actually hit it off, turning myth into reality? So what if she'd kind of decided to take the serious route and be a full-time student next year? That was next year, and the rest of this year was all about having fun, fun, fun. Who knew—she might even change her mind, defer her admission, become a Raves groupie, and tour with the band for the next five years!

And only just a moment ago she was all pleased with herself for being so decisive.

Serena bit her nails for a few seconds, then hit reply and typed three letters using only her partially chewed-on, partially pink-polished index finger.

Y-E-S.

an unlikely match

Blair trolled the Internet for the exquisite Jimmy Choo shoes she'd seen in *W* but had yet to find in her size. They were made of green silk, hand-sewn with tiny mother-of-pearl hearts all over the heels. They'd only distributed three hundred pairs of the shoes worldwide, but surely there had to be one size-seven-and-a-half that hadn't been claimed—in Mexico City, maybe, or Hong Kong, where feet tended to be small.

Next to her, Vanessa Abrams was furiously typing, building some sort of feminist Web page or something. Blair glanced at her neighbor's screen. *Roommate Wanted*, she read in big, bold letters. *Female Only*.

Blair had never been too fond of her shaven-headed, black-wearing, film auteur classmate. Every word Vanessa uttered in class was said with an air of I'm-only-talking-to-you-because-you-asked-me-a-question, like she was so much smarter and more astute than even the teachers. And she'd always suspected that Vanessa preferred girls to boys.

"I interviewed this guy this weekend. Turned out to be a serious weirdo."

Blair glanced at her neighbor and discovered that Vanessa was actually addressing her.

"I decided to stick with female applicants only," Vanessa added, clicking the enter button on her keyboard for emphasis.

Blair pressed her lips together and shifted in her chair. Vanessa really did seem to be talking to her. "I met a guy this weekend, too," she confessed. She bit her lip and pointed to Vanessa's screen. "Why do you want a roommate anyway? I'd kill to live on my own."

Vanessa shrugged her shoulders. It was weird enough conversing with bitchy Blair Waldorf, but even weirder still that Blair's question was actually worth thinking about.

"My sister's on tour in Europe. I don't know, I guess I get lonely," Vanessa admitted before she could stop herself. As soon as she'd said it she felt like clamping her hand over her mouth. Why would Blair Waldorf of all people even *care*?

"What about your boyfriend—that geek—?" Blair bit her lip and corrected herself. "That boy with the . . . notebook."

"We broke up."

Blair nodded, tempted to explain how she'd just broken up with her boyfriend, and how sometimes she felt lonely too. Discreetly, she sized Vanessa up. She kind of liked how Vanessa didn't gush about what a loser her ex-boyfriend was, complaining about the gifts he'd given her, imitating the stupid way he tied his shoes, and reiterating the whole sad saga. Vanessa was weird, but at least she wasn't predictable. And it was well known that Vanessa's parents lived in Vermont, so if her sister was away, she really was all on her own.

"So how does it work?" Blair asked. "Are you, like, interviewing prospective roommates?"

Vanessa had to wonder where all this was going.

"Well, first I screen them through Instant Messenger, and if they sound normal I interview them. But so far, no one's been normal."

Blair couldn't believe she was even considering living with lesbo, baldo, weirdo, no-friends Vanessa, but she really did need a place to live. Her own home was intolerable, and after her run-in with Mrs. M this morning, she was pretty sure she couldn't live at the Plaza for the rest of the school year without completely ruining her chances of getting into Yale. And what if she needed to entertain . . . a guest? An apartment without parents or nannies or maids or cooks was the *perfect* place, even if it had to be in dirty, disgusting Williamsburg. She might even convince Vanessa to hire a decorator, and introduce some color to the apartment. Not that she had actually seen Vanessa's place, but after going to school with her for the last one hundred years, she was pretty sure the apartment was done entirely in black. She could make the place over completely, just like the frumpy, bookish Audrey Hepburn was made over into a fabulous fashion model in *My Fair Lady*!

"Interview me," she suggested.

"But—" Vanessa countered. "I live in *Brooklyn*."

Blair twisted her ruby ring around and around on the ring finger of her left hand. "I *know*." She sighed mournfully down at her black patent leather flats and closed her eyes, trying to picture herself as a hip, artsy Williamsburg person. She'd wear drab green T-shirts with ironic decals on them like WILLIAMSBURG IS FOR LOVERS. She'd take her coffee black. She'd wear Converse sneakers without socks and carry a vintage purple plastic handbag. She'd get orange highlights and wear black octagonally framed glasses. She'd eat falafel. She'd write poetry. She'd get a lip ring and a tattoo! Oh, wouldn't Nate just die. A smile spread across her face. "I've always wanted to live in Brooklyn."

Yeah, right.

"No, you—" Vanessa began in an attempt to dissuade her.

"You have cable, TiVo, and a DVD player, right?" Blair demanded.

Wait, who's supposed to interview who?

"I *have* to watch my movies," Blair insisted, like a TV-dinner-eating old biddy who couldn't survive without her daily dose of Regis and Kelly.

"Movies?" Vanessa repeated, wondering if Blair had completely lost her mind. She'd forgotten that Blair was a huge old movie fan. Back in November, Blair had even entered a film contest at school. All she'd done was replay the first ten minutes of *Breakfast at Tiffany*'s over and over to different music, because in her opinion it was the perfect first ten minutes of any film *ever*. Vanessa had won the contest with her version of *War and Peace*, starring her former best friend Dan Humphrey as the dying Prince Andrei. That had been before they'd even kissed—what seemed like a century ago.

"Anything starring Audrey Hepburn. Or Jimmy Stewart. Or Cary Grant. Or Lauren Bacall." Blair clarified breathlessly. "And of course, *Gone with the Wind*."

If there was one thing Vanessa had plenty of, it was film equipment, TVs, videos, and DVDs. "Don't worry. I'm majoring in film at NYU next year. I have everything," Vanessa assured her. "All the classics."

"And how do you get to school?" Blair demanded, wondering if she might have to learn to drive. Keeping her eyes on her computer screen, she wiggled her mouse to give the impression that she was hard at work. "Isn't there, like, some bridge you have to cross?"

Considering that Manhattan is an island, then yes, probably a bridge would be involved.

Vanessa decided to humor her. Not that Blair Waldorf

really wanted to live in her dodgy, graffitied Brooklyn apartment building with its view of other dodgy, graffitied Brooklyn apartment buildings. "The L train goes to Union Square and then I change to the 6."

Huh?

Blair frowned. Was she talking about the *subway*?

"If the weather's really bad or I'm really late, I call a car service," Vanessa admitted.

Aha!

"And do you mind . . . you know, *visitors*?" Blair asked.

As in *male* visitors?

Vanessa laughed. "As long as they don't smell and they bring food."

Blair nodded seriously. She'd have her very own apartment in which to have wild and crazy sex with Stan 5 or any other boy she chose, and she would turn herself into the sexiest, most pierced and tattooed girl in Williamsburg. Nate would go absolutely crazy with regret. "I think this could work out, don't you?"

Vanessa's brown eyes had ceased blinking. "But we hate each other," she said matter-of-factly.

Blair rolled her eyes and knocked her tanned bony knee against Vanessa's pale round one. "Oh, don't be such a snob," she huffed, really getting into her new role as Vanessa's long-lost hipster sister. "Now, about your boyfriend problem," she continued, as if the matter was already closed. "The thing is, and no offense, but I bet you're only attracted to guys who are kind of 'alternative,' like you—" Blair clamped her mouth shut, as her brain underwent a lightbulb moment. Why she'd never thought of it before she didn't know, but her dread-locked so-called alternative stepbrother Aaron and the shaven-headed, black-wearing Vanessa were *absolutely* the perfect couple! They could paint each other's toenails black, cook vegan sushi, film each other's hair or lack thereof, and otherwise entertain themselves while she was busy seducing the boy who was going to get her into Yale.

See, maybe Williamsburg really *is* for lovers!

gossipgirl.co.uk

topics ◀ *previous* **next** ▶ *post a question* **reply**

Disclaimer: All the real names of places, people, and events have been altered or abbreviated to protect the innocent. Namely, me.

hey people!

The odd couple

Who would've thunk it? A girl married to her eight-hundred-dollar Manolos has tentatively moved in with a classmate who has never worn anything on her feet but steel-toed Doc Marten boots and black Danskin kneesocks. One thing is for sure, they won't be sharing clothes. But since they come from two entirely different planets, they definitely have a lot to talk about and a lot to learn. A sample conversation:

"Have you seen the brush for my Stila bronzing powder?"

"Oh, are you doing an art project?"

I'm taking bets for how long this crazy sleepover is going to last!

Quel désastre!

Word also has it that a certain French tie-dye-wearing hippie chick has told the entire world that she and our favorite stoner lacrosse jock aren't just seeing each other—they're in *love*. Uh-oh.

Your e-mail

Dear GG,
I volunteer in the admissions office at my college, which happens to be one of the Ivies, and my friends and I have spent a lot of time courting this one incoming freshman because we think she'd be the perfect pledge for our sorority. She's gorgeous and smart and talented—just like we are. The thing is, she hasn't

answered a single one of our e-mails. I know it sounds corny, but what if we sent her, like, a care package or something—do you think it would help?
—PrincetonBabe

Dear PrincetonBabe,
I hate to break it to you, but I don't think so.
—GG

Sightings

C at Tower Records buying a pirated version of the latest Raves single starring none other than **D**, who is supposedly his least-favorite person of all time. Is it the music or the words that he can't resist? **K** and **I** sampling acne-clearing Origins products at the Madison Avenue store and inadvertently slipping a few freebies into their Tod's bags when the sales assistant turned her back. **B** and **V** plying the grocery store delivery man with a box of Godiva truffles to get him to carry their shopping bags up three flights to their apartment door. And were those black-and-white toile curtains with balloon valances we saw in the windows? Guess they're *both* learning to compromise!

The calm before the storm

This week I've actually witnessed my classmates hanging around in front of school after it gets out, chatting about their summer plans, and drinking iced lattes. A few weeks ago we were skipping class to sunbathe in the park, listening to our MP3s, and barely speaking to one another. Now we don't know what to do with ourselves, and we can't stand to be alone. Chalk it up to the cloudy, humid, airless May weather, and the fact that in less than four weeks some of us will never see each other again. I'm also convinced that something's cooking. Just watch: Come Friday, all hell will break loose.

I'll be there with bells on!

You know you love me,

s is unimpressed

A nice-sized trust fund from his great-grandfather, who was involved in the invention of Velcro, and the money from the Raves' bestselling first album, *Jimmy and Jane*, had bought twenty-three-year-old Damian Polk a cute four-story white town house with red shutters on quaint Bedford Street in the West Village. Bedford Street was only three blocks long, dotted with intimate restaurants, cozy cafés, historic houses, a famous speakeasy, and gorgeous gay men walking their toy dogs. Outside, the house looked like an antique dollhouse, but inside it was a showplace for modern, minimalist white furniture. Rumor had it that although Damian wore all sorts of colors onstage, he never wore anything but white inside his house, and never allowed his guests to wear anything but white either, not even blue jeans.

Too bad he forgot to tell certain people that particular rule.

The front door was standing open, and Serena climbed the white marble steps to the second floor, wearing her favorite pair of Blue Cult flares, a cropped hot pink T-shirt, and a crazy pair of Hollywould hot pink platform flip-flops that were a challenge to walk in. She could hear some sort of psychedelic jazz music playing, the clink of glasses, and the murmur of voices.

Jenny Humphrey was sitting cross-legged on the white lacquered countertop of the island in Damian's white open kitchen, drinking a glass of milk. Her hair was in pigtails and she was wearing a white cotton undershirt and white cotton boxer shorts.

"Hey!" she cried, bouncing off the counter to greet Serena. "Damian said you were coming. He's in the shower." She tiptoed over in her bare feet and tilted her lily white chin up to kiss Serena's cheek. "I'm so glad you're here."

Well, *hello*, little hostess to the mostest! What a change from the Jenny who only last week was completely gaga at the opportunity to be invited into Serena's home. And wasn't she like *banned* from hanging out with the Raves ever again?

As if that made any difference.

"I snuck out," Jenny whispered. "Dad was watching some totally boring Allen Ginsberg documentary. He thinks I'm in my room, like, *painting* or something."

Ah, painting. It used to be her only pastime, back when she was young and innocent.

Serena smiled down at her petite, curly-haired protégé, feeling oddly out of place. The other party-goers lounged on the white suede sectional sofa in the vaulted white living room adjoining the kitchen, dressed head-to-toe in white, drinking giant gin martinis with hard-boiled eggs floating in them. One wall of the living room was decorated with white paper snowflake cut-outs like the kind you make in kindergarten, and another wall was painted to look like bookshelves filled with white books.

Because real books are too colorful?

A tall skinny guy was sitting on a wooly white polar bear

rug, wearing only a white terrycloth bathrobe. A huge brown-and-black dog lay beside him, its enormous brown-and-black head buried in his lap—the only bit of color in an entirely white room.

"Ooh la la!" Jenny chirped giddily as Damian appeared, still damp from the shower and wearing nothing but a pair of white cashmere sweatpants. His reddish blond hair was still damp, and drops of water had collected in the indentations of his collarbone. His arms and chest were covered with tiny freckles and big muscles, and yes, he was even more good-looking in person than on his album covers.

"Hello," Serena greeted him, feeling uncharacteristically starstruck. And how come no one had told her about the all-white dress code? Was she just supposed to *know*?

"Now I know why everyone said I had to meet you," he said automatically when he saw Serena.

Serena blushed at the compliment, but she couldn't think of anything to say. A rare occasion for her—the van der Woodsens were bred to say the right thing at the right time at all times.

Jenny took Serena's hand and then Damian's, standing between them like a buxom flower girl at an arranged marriage. "You have to show Serena your bedroom," she told Damian. She turned to Serena. "His bedroom is *so* cool."

Yeah? How would she know?

Damian shrugged and starting walking into the living room, pulling Jenny and Serena along with him. "Come, sit down. Kelly and Ping should be here any minute."

"Cool," Serena responded, although she had no idea who he was talking about. Kelly and Ping—were they another band? A clown act? DJs?

"Yum. They have the *best* pad Thai *ever*," Jenny said, like she'd been ordering from the SoHo Asian eatery all her life.

"Yum," Serena agreed. What was wrong with her? She wasn't even hungry.

Jenny broke away from them and perched on some guy's knee. He had dark hair and dimpled cheeks and was wearing white painter's overalls, looking every bit like the Raves' drummer, Lloyd Collins.

Cuz that's exactly who he *was*.

"Hi Serena," Lloyd greeted her in that taunting, cocky way of his. "I feel like we're sisters already," he added, flapping his wrists and pretending to be Damian's long-lost gay twin.

"Damian just made a recording of me singing 'Happy Birthday to Me.' He's going to sample it on the band's next track," Jenny announced gaily to anyone who was listening. "I can't wait for Dan to hear it."

"Isn't he here?" Serena asked, looking around for the cloud of Camel smoke that usually engulfed Dan Humphrey's head.

"Not yet," Damian replied, and Serena thought she detected a note of malice in his voice.

Dan and Serena had gotten together that fall, but it had been short-lived—just like all of her relationships—and they hadn't exactly stayed in touch. But there were no hard feelings, and it might be nice to hang out and be friends now that they were both graduating. She wondered where he was going to college next year, or if he was going to take some time off to tour with the band.

"Cigar?" Damian asked, holding a box out to her. "They came in from Cuba last night."

"Breadstick?" Lloyd asked, flipping a breadstick up in the air like one of his drumsticks and catching it in his teeth. "They're Italian and supercrisp."

"No, thanks," Serena responded quietly to both offers. Here she was, a notorious party girl at what was bound to become a notorious party, yet she felt completely uninspired. Maybe the fact that everyone thought she and Damian were already together was ruining it for her. Or maybe seeing Jenny, the image of herself two or three years ago, was making her realize that she was ready to try something new. Or maybe it was because these were the very last weeks of her senior year, before the summer, and before Yale. She didn't care so much about meeting rock stars; she just wanted to hang out with her friends.

Blair was at Vanessa's apartment in Williamsburg right now—probably wallpapering the bathroom with little pink rosebuds or something—and there was no place Serena would rather be.

"Mind if I use your bathroom?" she asked.

Damian directed her through a set of white velvet drapes and down a long white corridor to a white-tiled, mirror-ceilinged, marble-bathed bathroom. Serena closed the door, yanked her tube of MAC Cherry Ice lip gloss from her back pocket, and smeared some on. Down the corridor, on the other side of the white velvet drapes, came the sounds of the doorbell ringing and Kelly and Ping delivering their Asian delicacies. She pushed opened the bathroom door again and hurried down the corridor, slipping past the cluster of arriving caterers and out onto the steamy sidewalk once more.

This from a girl known for dancing on tables in bars throughout France? This from the girl who'd had an unmentionable part of her body photographed and plastered on the sides of buses and in subways all over the city? Ditching a party before it even got started?

Then again, it didn't really matter whether she stayed at the party or not. Whatever Serena did was bound to make headlines.

the odd couple

"So, this drawer is where we'll keep all our cleansers, moisturizers, toners, exfoliators, masks, and makeup removers. All the bath gel is in the bottom drawer, closest to the tub. And see? That's an Egyptian cotton bath rug to cover that icky gray linoleum tile." Blair pointed to the new peach-colored rug that she'd just installed in Vanessa's bathroom.

Vanessa pulled open the drawers in the cracked, cream-colored vanity beneath the bathroom sink. Everything had been alphabetized and color-coded to Blair's control-freak specifications. Not that Vanessa owned any beauty products herself. It was all Blair's stuff anyway.

"You can borrow whatever you want," Blair offered generously. She pulled out a tiny porcelain jar of La Mer eye cream and started dabbing some under her eyes. "This stuff is amazing," she declared, "I just wish it didn't smell like cold cream." She reached out and dabbed some under Vanessa's eyes. One application wouldn't do much, but if she could get Vanessa to use it once a day, in a week those eggplant-sized puffs would be totally gone. Maybe Vanessa would even let her do a total makeover on her. They could go jeans shopping together at Bloomingdale's SoHo, and even buy Vanessa a nice wig!

Nice try.

"Where's my shaver?" Vanessa grumbled, twisting her face away from Blair like a kid who hates to have her face cleaned. "I have to reshave my head like once a week, you know."

"Shavers?" Blair repeated cluelessly. She pointed to a bag of trash slumped against the door outside the bathroom. "I think they might be in there." She grabbed an eyebrow brush from out of a freshly organized drawer and ran it over Vanessa's prickly head stubble. "Have you ever thought about maybe growing it—?"

"*No!*" Vanessa told her adamantly, swiping the eyebrow brush away. She dumped the bag of trash out onto the peach-colored carpet and rescued her electric shaver, placing it in the top vanity drawer next to Blair's eyelash curlers.

"Sorry," Blair allowed. "I should have asked first."

"That's okay." Vanessa fingered the eyelash curlers curiously. "What the fuck are these anyway?"

Blair snatched them up eagerly and sat Vanessa down on top of the toilet seat. "Don't close your eyes. And don't worry, this doesn't hurt." She held the curlers an inch away from Vanessa's lashes, squinting. Then she put them down again. "You know what?" she told her new roommate. "You don't need these. Your lashes are thick and curly." She squinted again, as if she couldn't quite believe it. "In fact, they're completely *perfect.*"

Vanessa stood up and examined her eyelashes in the bathroom mirror, feeling extremely flattered, although she'd never have admitted it. "Can we get something to eat now, goddammit? We've been redecorating all goddamned day."

For once Blair had been so preoccupied, she hadn't even thought about food. Tonight would be her first night in the apartment, and she'd spent the whole afternoon unpacking and organizing. What did Vanessa usually do for dinner, she wondered. *Cook?*

The two girls wandered out of the bathroom and into the open kitchen, surveying the apartment with their hands on their hips. Blair's mother's baby nursery decorator had sent her team of painters over on Wednesday and Thursday while Vanessa was at school, and the whole apartment had been redone in shades of celery green and dove gray—nothing too girly, so as not to offend Vanessa. After school on Thursday, Vanessa had discovered a set of used curtains at Domsey's that she could actually tolerate, even though they were covered in an exotic-bird-and-palm-leaf-print toile, because they were black and white. And this morning the decorator had scheduled a delivery of six twentieth-century modern wooden chairs, a small oval dining table, a cool kidney bean–shaped Noguchi glass coffee table, and two gray suede beanbag chairs, which Blair and Vanessa kept moving around the living room just because it was fun.

"I can't believe I'm saying this, but I like it," Vanessa admitted.

"Really?" Blair asked cautiously. It was kind of a major transformation, and she wouldn't have been surprised if Vanessa had kicked her out before she'd even unpacked her Louis Vuitton suitcases.

"We could have a dinner party," Vanessa mused. She walked over to the oval-shaped birch dining table and readjusted the six funky birch swivel chairs surrounding it. "Except I don't have anyone to invite."

Nobody did a party better than Blair Waldorf. Even if it was just a chic little bohemian Brooklyn dinner party.

Blair whipped her cell phone out of her James jeans pocket and speed-dialed Serena's number. "Unless you and that rock star dude are, like, in bed already, wanna come to dinner at my new place?"

"I'm already on my way over," Serena told her. "Sorry to disappoint you, though—I'm on my own."

Then Blair called Stan 5. "What took you so long?" he wanted to know.

And she called her stepbrother, Aaron. "What are you cooking?" he asked suspiciously. "Should I bring over some tempeh?"

Blair hadn't exactly worked out the food part. "We can order from Nobu." She put her hand over the mouthpiece. "Do they even have Nobu in Brooklyn?"

Vanessa waved a pizza menu in her face, and Blair saw that there was something called the Cheeseless Paradise Pie under vegetarian selections. "Don't worry," she told her stepbrother. "I've got you covered."

"So what's Vanessa like exactly?" Aaron asked curiously.

Blair grinned devilishly. "That's for me to know and you to find out."

even french girls get dissed

"Allo?" Lexie's distinct French-accented English rang out over Nate's intercom. "Mayee I pleeze come up?"

Locked in his room all week with a bong, playing Grand Theft Auto San Andreas on his Xbox, Nate hadn't received any visitors except Jeremy, Anthony, and Charlie, who stopped by every now and then to replenish his stash and fill him in on what was going on at school. His wing of the house smelled like half-eaten burritos, spilled bong water, and pizza-flavored Pepperidge Farm goldfish—not that there was anyone around to smell it. After grounding him, his parents had taken the *Charlotte* up the Hudson to visit friends in Kingston and to ensure that Nate didn't steal the boat again before their benefit cruise. If only he hadn't messed things up with Blair, they'd have had the whole house to themselves and could have had sex on top of the grand piano in the living room if they'd wanted.

Oh, well.

"I'm sick," he lied into the intercom. "It's really contagious. I've missed the whole week of school."

"It's okay, I'm sick too!" Lexie responded brightly. She coughed to demonstrate just how sick she really was. "We can share our germs!"

What fun!

Nate had just heisted a Hummer, but when Lexie buzzed he'd gotten distracted and the cops had gone right up his ass. He kicked the Xbox controls across the room and licked his bong-chapped lips. His mouth felt like it was coated with pot-flavored road tar, and he hadn't changed his shirt in who knew how many days.

"I smell," he confided into the speaker. "Seriously. It's bad."

"We'll 'av a bath," Lexie told him gaily. "Buzz me in. I'll give you a mah-ssage, bay-bee," she added, sounding even more French than she'd sounded only a moment ago.

Nate could tell she wasn't going to give up, and it wasn't like Blair wasn't cheating on him right then too. Besides, Lexie was hot and obviously desperate for it, and he was seriously bored.

"Okay," he replied slowly, about to press the buzzer to let her in.

"Oh, I love you!" Lexie cried into the intercom.

Nate blinked slowly. Did she say *love*? He let his hand drop. Girls—all they ever seemed to do was fall in love with him and get him into trouble. Blair, Serena, Jennifer, Georgie, and now this horny, fake-accented, hippie French chick, Lexie.

Wait, is this, like, *another* epiphany?

The thing was, he was about to graduate and go off to Yale. He wanted to hang out with the girls he'd grown up with and always known and loved. Not some new chick.

Especially not one who didn't even speak the same language.

"Look, I'm grounded," he said firmly. "Go home."

"Mais non!" Lexie wailed, starting to cry.

Mais oui.

will s own up or chicken out?

The door to Vanessa and Blair's apartment stood open. Serena stepped inside, her freshly glossed mouth agape at how changed it was since Vanessa's birthday party. Only a few weeks ago there had been black sheets hanging in the windows and plaster crumbling onto the barely furnished floors. Now it was freshly painted and filled with cool modern furniture. Lemongrass-scented candles burned on the coffee table, and cool black-and-white toile curtains billowed from the open windows in the living room.

"Whoa," she gasped.

"I know," Vanessa called over from the open kitchen where she was busy filling little ceramic bowls with Greek olives, baby carrots, and tamari-roasted almonds so their guests would have something to munch on before the pizza arrived. "Can you believe it?" She thrust her pale leg into the air and waggled her foot so Serena could see that she'd borrowed Blair's wedge-soled black patent leather Sigerson Morrison Mary Janes. "Like my shoes?"

Blair padded barefoot out of the bedroom with an empty tumbler of ice in her hand, looking very Williamsburg in a tight black T-shirt, a short black Seven jeans skirt, and mod silvery pink lipstick. She kissed Serena's cheek. "Isn't it great?" she asked, looking genuinely thrilled.

While her cab idled in traffic on the Williamsburg Bridge on the ride over, Serena had geared herself up to tell Blair that she'd decided to go to Yale next year. But now that they were face-to-face, she could feel herself chickening out.

She dipped her hand into Blair's glass and stole a vodka tonic–soaked ice cube. "I hope you took before and after pictures."

"Don't worry." Vanessa stomped out of the kitchen in Blair's shoes and handed Serena a vodka tonic of her own. "I even got the painters' butt cracks."

Of course she did.

The three girls sat down on Ruby's old futon sofa, which had been refurbished with a new birch frame and a new gray faux-suede cover.

"So what happened with Damian?" Blair wanted to know. "I thought we were going to be reading about you guys in the paper tomorrow."

Serena rolled the legs of her jeans up to her bony knees. "Well, he's good-looking and everything, but . . ." She hesitated and rolled her pant legs back down again. Then she took a sip of her drink and quickly changed the subject. "Who else is coming over tonight anyway?"

Blair bit her lip. It hadn't really occurred to her that Serena might ever be the odd one out. "You're not going to like this, but I kind of invited that Stanford Parris kid from the Yale party? And Aaron—you know, my stepbrother? I think he and Vanessa are, like, *made* for each other."

Vanessa took a huge gulp of her rum and Coke. "We'll see," she belched loudly.

Serena's huge, dark blue eyes shone as she digested this

information. She'd actually been in love with Aaron for a week or two that winter, but enough time had passed now that she could handle hanging out with him on a just-friends basis. And Blair was right—Vanessa and Aaron *were* perfect for each other. "Cool," she told her friend graciously, even though she really had thought that Stan 5 guy was a conceited jerk.

The downstairs buzzer rang and Blair and Vanessa both shot out of their seats and bolted to the window overlooking the street. Aaron Rose and Stanford Parris V were standing on the sidewalk, each looking dubiously up at the second-floor apartment.

"Oh my God, they're here!" the oddly paired roommates squealed in unison.

All of a sudden Serena felt like the chaperone at a junior-high sleepover party. She rolled her eyes. "Do you girls want me to get the door so you can go fix your hair or something?" she offered jokingly.

"Yes, please!" Blair cried. She grabbed Vanessa's arm and dragged her toward the bathroom.

Serena chewed on a piece of ice and pressed play on Vanessa's CD player as she waited for the boys to mount the stairs. The Raves song "Ice Cream" came on and she quickly selected the next disc—one of Ruby's weird German disco albums.

Someone knocked on the door and she hurried over to answer it. Now if they could just avoid the topic of college for the rest of the evening . . .

Not likely.

way to alienate your sister
and lose your job

Dan would have been perfectly happy eating sushi with
Monique and taking in an old French film down at that artsy
movie theater on Twelfth Street. But Monique had insisted
that they could slip into Damian's party unnoticed, steal a
bottle of champagne and a few cigars, and then creep out
onto one of the fire escapes and have a party of their own.

Bedford Street was exactly the kind of über-cool, exclusive, West Village neighborhood Dan envisioned himself living
in when he became an absurdly famous rock star, and it felt
extremely cool to swagger down the street with gorgeous
Monique on his arm. She was wearing an ankle-length, completely see-through, white silk sundress and white sandals,
and he was wearing his favorite pair of worn-in rust-colored
corduroys and a soft black T-shirt. He thought they looked
pretty good together.

Guess no one told him about the white thing either.

The door to Damian's town house was standing open and
the scent of shrimp pad Thai wafted out of it. Before they
reached the top of the white marble steps, Dan distinctly
heard the voice of his sister, Jenny. And she wasn't talking—
she was *singing*.

Happy birthday to me, happy birthday to me!

Dan let go of Monique's hand and blinked in the bright whiteness. His fingers trembled and his palms began to sweat. Damian's entire place was white, white, white. Even the other guests at the party were wearing white. Sure, it was cool. He just wished someone had told him.

Jenny's voice continued to blare out of the stereo.

Happy birthday to me, happy birthday to me!

"Hey," Dan called unevenly. He walked over to where Jenny sat on the white sectional sofa, her butt in Lloyd's lap and her calves resting on Damian's knees. "What's going on? Dad told me you were spending the weekend up at Elise's country house."

Jenny giggled, obviously enthralled with her own craftiness. "Elise *is* in the country." She giggled and leaned back against Lloyd's chest. "But I'm *here*. Dad's so totally gullible."

Dan didn't like the idea of Jenny lying to their dad. Sure, he'd told his share of harmless untruths, but little sisters were supposed to be pure and innocent and true, not lying schemers who sat on older guys' laps, flirting their heads off while dressed in flimsy, see-through white undershirts and a pair of some guy's boxer shorts. He would have written a poem about how she kind of reminded him of Ophelia, except he was too friggin' pissed off.

"With doz breasts, you must get away with murder!" Monique pointed at Jenny's barely clad boobs.

Dan's hands were shaking uncontrollably now. He reached for the pack of Camels in his back pocket and thrust one in his mouth. "I don't even know what you're doing here," he growled at his sister with the unlit cigarette between his teeth. "This is *my* band," he added, sounding completely immature.

Damian raised his nicely arched strawberry blond eyebrows. "Actually, Jenny is singing for us now."

Dan waited for Damian to bust into a fit of giggles and tell him he was joking, but Damian kept a straight face.

"Dad's always saying I need a job to support my shopping habit," Jenny gushed, her face shiny with excitement and full of adorable dimples.

"And we decided we need a softer sound," Lloyd added, stroking Jenny's curly hair. "Of course, we'll still use your songs. Just with Jennifer's voice."

Excusez-moi?

Dan lit his cigarette with his neon green plastic Bic and tossed the lighter on the white sofa out of sheer rebellion. The way Damian was holding Jenny's bare feet while not wearing a shirt over his well-developed, manly chest was totally infuriating.

Damian eyed Monique warily. "I thought you went back to St. Barts, sweetie."

Monique grinned. "Vell, I have been trying to get Dan to go there with me, but he says he has to finish school first." She rolled her eyes. "*Boring.*"

"Serena van der Woodsen was here," Jenny told her brother. "But she left. Not that you care."

"And she's prettier than you, Monique," Lloyd added bitchily. He squeezed Jenny around the waist. "But not nearly as cute as you, dumplin'."

Dan sucked furiously on his cigarette, trying desperately not to scream his fucking head off. It would have been nice to see Serena, but he kind of had other things on his mind. "Uh, Damian, could I talk to you for a minute?" he demanded between gritted teeth.

"Ciao, ciao, darling!" Monique called to someone across the room and drifted away from Dan to smother a bald Moby look-alike in a white linen tracksuit with her wet, pine nut–scented kisses.

Dan waited for Damian to remove his hands from Jenny's feet, stand up, put a shirt on, and talk to him in private, like a man.

Yeah.

But Damian stayed where he was. "Anything you need to say can be said in front of Lloyd and your big sister. We're all family, right?"

Big sister?

Dan's free hand closed in a sweaty fist. "Jenny's not my big sister," he hissed. "I'm turning eighteen in two weeks. She'll be fifteen in July."

"Thanks a lot!" Jenny complained.

Damian and Lloyd's eyes bulged a little bit, but they didn't say anything. Then Lloyd cracked a grin. "Well, at least she's not married."

Damian elbowed him in the ribs. "I'll handle this." He pulled a tiny bottle of Stoli out of his back pocket and took a swig. His red-blond hair was shorter than it had been only a week ago, and more stylishly tousled.

Maybe that was because he had it cut by Sally Hershberger only yesterday?

"Dan," Damian continued. "You sang like shit last Saturday. And you basically threw up onstage. Then you hooked up with my wife."

Wife?

Dan's stomach dropped. Monique had never said anything about being anyone's *wife*. He had a sudden urge to take a very long cold shower.

"We're estranged," Damian clarified.

Oh, well, that's a relief.

"I respect your words, yeah?" Damian told him solemnly. "But I'm just not feeling the love."

Dan shifted his gaze to the other party guests—visions of coolness and sophistication, wearing white designer clothes, happily quaffing their boiled-egg martinis and munching on shrimp shu mai and rice noodles, their hair as shiny and Sally Hershberger–groovy as Damian's. Dan wore corduroys from Old Navy and got a haircut at Supercuts once a year. He liked instant coffee and hot dogs bought on the street. He liked coming home in the evenings and laughing at the local news with his dad. His bedroom had linty maroon wall-to-wall carpeting that he was actually sort of fond of. He only owned two pairs of shoes. He was never meant to be a rock star.

"Come on, Jenny. Let's go home." He held a grim hand out to his little sister.

Jenny glared at him. Was he crazy? The guys in the Raves didn't even mind that she was only fourteen. She was definitely staying. "You go home," she challenged.

Dan flapped a sweaty hand at her. "We can get a cab. I'll pay."

Jenny shrank away from him, her back pressed against Lloyd's chest. "Please don't be an idiot, Dan," she yawned dismissively. "And don't say anything to Dad. I'll deal with him on my own."

"Fine." Dan shoved his hands in his pockets. He had a feeling Jenny sort of wanted to get into trouble with their dad, but he wasn't going to tell on her. She was doing fine in the trouble department all on her own. "If you think I'm going to give you any of my poems, though, you can forget about it."

Damian raised his eyebrows, Lloyd rolled his eyes, and Jenny kicked at the white sofa with her bare feet—as if they were all completely bored with Dan's little tirade. Across the room Monique was eating noodles right out of the serving dish with a pair of ivory-lacquered chopsticks. A girl in a white embroidered bolero jacket who looked a lot like Chloë Sevigny was braiding Monique's long, honey-colored hair while she ate.

"Tell your wife I said good-bye," Dan grumbled at Damian. He hesitated, giving Jenny one last chance to leave with him, but she'd shifted around on Lloyd's lap so her back was to him.

"'Bye, Dan," she said, sounding like she couldn't wait for him to be gone.

Dan shuffled down the white marble steps and out onto Bedford Street, unsure whether to laugh or to cry. It was kind of a relief knowing he'd never have to sing onstage again. He could go to college, be a normal kid, have a normal girlfriend, and a normal life.

Whatever that meant.

truth or dare

Blair remained in the bathroom, preparing for her entrance, leaving Vanessa to hang back near the kitchen like a shy thirteen-year-old while Serena answered the door. Vanessa felt like a total dweeb wearing Blair's supershiny lip gloss and the one pair of black stretch Levis she'd stopped wearing over a year ago because she'd decided they were too tight. In fact, she felt like a total dweeb, period. Aaron would probably be a complete snob who though she was a fat, bald weirdo, just like Blair had always thought before she'd lost her mind and decided to move in with her.

"Hey." Aaron stepped into the apartment and kissed Serena on the cheek. "You live here too?" He was wearing an orange hemp wifebeater T-shirt, his usual army-issue pants, and black cruelty-free rubber flip-flops. He'd pinned his dark dreadlocks back with two turquoise heart-shaped barrettes stolen out of Blair's bathroom, obviously trying to gauge Vanessa's vegan-freak tolerance by looking as vegan-freaky as possible.

Serena was relieved to discover that she really was over him. "Oh, no. I'm just here to open the door."

Stan 5 towered blondly in the hall carrying two large

pizza boxes in his arms, looking like a prep-school poster boy in a khaki Hugo Boss suit, a pink Brooks Brothers shirt, and a Kelly-green-and-pink-striped Turnbull & Asser tie. "The delivery guy was downstairs," he said, looking bewildered. "It sure is different here," he added, making it very clear that he had never been to Brooklyn in his entire life.

"Hello again," Serena said. "I guess you two have already met." She took the pizzas and carried them into the kitchen. Stan 5 hovered near Aaron, his eyes searching the tiny apartment for the girl who'd actually invited him there.

Heartened by the sight of Aaron's ridiculous hairstyle, Vanessa ventured forward a few steps. "Hi!" she greeted them, wishing she didn't sound so perky and dumb. "I'm Vanessa."

Aaron smiled, and she immediately liked his thin red lips and the way his dark, almost black eyes shone in the candle-light. He walked over and shook her hand. He was skinny, and slightly taller than she was. Five-foot-nine, maybe—the same height as Dan—but Aaron seemed bigger, more ath-letic. He pointed at her feet. "Hey, those are Blair's shoes, aren't they? My dog tried to eat those for breakfast once."

"Not that she'd notice. She has about eight hundred pairs," Vanessa observed.

They chuckled, grinning at each other. A regular mutual admiration society.

Serena was about to go and drag Blair out of the bath-room when Blair reappeared in a cloud of Carolina Herrera perfume, her eyelashes freshly curled, her hair reparted, and her face dusted with sparkly, rose-tinted bronzing powder. She was still wearing the same tight black T-shirt, but she'd put on a different bra and her chest looked more like a C now than a B.

"Who wants a drink?" she asked, smiling coyly at Stan 5.

"I'd love one," Stan 5 replied. He walked over and kissed her on the cheek. He was taller than she remembered, and more formal. But he smelled like Polo for Men, which was one of her favorites.

Blair batted her curly-lashed eyes at him. *I'm going to seduce you tonight,* she told him silently.

Serena couldn't stand how weird everyone was being. Besides, it was almost ten o'clock—way past her dinnertime. She flipped open the lid of one of the pizza boxes. "Mind if we eat now? I'm starving."

Vanessa and Aaron each took a vegan slice and a rum and Coke and sat down at the table. Blair refreshed her drink and slipped a huge cheesy pepperoni slice onto her plate, thinking that she was going to need her energy. Stan 5 took two pepperoni slices—obviously he thought he was going to need his energy too. And Serena took one of each, because she'd always been a big eater.

"Why don't we play a game or something?" she suggested once they were seated around the table. Normally she wouldn't have cared, but right now she'd do anything to stop them all from smiling at each other so . . . moronically.

Blair took a huge bite of pizza and washed it down with vodka tonic. *"Yes!"* she agreed, practically screaming. "Truth or dare!"

Serena poked at her pizza. As long as she stuck with dares, she'd be fine.

Aaron folded his slice of pizza in half and took two enormous bites. Vanessa liked the way his cute little ears moved up and down when he chewed. "I'll start," he volunteered, wiping his mouth on a paper napkin. "Dare."

Blair shoved her pizza at him. Big rounds of pepperoni sat

on top of the greasy cheese. "That's easy. I dare you to eat this."

Aaron rolled his eyes. "No way. Truth, then."

Blair tried to think of a good question to ask him, but Vanessa beat him to it.

"Do you believe in love at first sight?" She kept her eyes focused on her pizza, picking the little green buds off a piece of broccoli to keep from blushing with shame for asking such a totally cheesy question.

Aaron's leg seemed to edge ever so slightly in her direction until the knee of his army pants very lightly grazed her jeans. He picked the rest of his pizza up and then put it down again without taking a bite. "Hell yes," he declared, his thin red lips spreading wide across his straight white teeth. "I do now."

Blair nudged Vanessa's foot underneath the table and Vanessa's entire head flushed the color of Constance Billard's maroon wool uniform. "I told you so," Blair mouthed with silent delight. She picked a piece of pepperoni off her slice and popped into her mouth. "Now me. Dare."

Everyone tried to think of a good one. The thing about dares was they were always something silly. Truths were always far more interesting.

Not necessarily.

"I dare you to kiss me," Stan 5 said quietly, pushing back his chair to give Blair access. "For five minutes."

How totally seventh grade.

"Fine." Blair stood up and pushed her dark hair behind her ears. Did he think she wouldn't kiss him unless he dared her to? Well, she was planning to do a lot more than kiss later on. She perched on his knee and wrapped her arms around his neck. A little blob of pizza sauce had collected in the corner of his mouth, and because she'd drunk just a wee bit too much and eaten her pizza a wee bit too fast, the sight of it made her gag. She closed her eyes and breathed in the scent of Polo for Men. "Someone start timing," she directed.

She pressed her lips against his, trying to relax and get into it, but it was hard, especially in front of an audience. Stan 5's lips were salty, unfamiliar, and weirdly wet. She was about to break away, just to catch her breath, when she remembered the time she and Nate were in a kissing contest at a party at Serena's house at the end of seventh grade. They went into Serena's walk-in closet and Serena stood outside and timed them while they made out. They lasted forty-seven minutes, but the truth was, they weren't really kissing the whole time. They were whispering ever so softly with their lips pressed together so it was almost like they were kissing when they were talking, and vice versa. Which was actually way more romantic.

"Time's up," Aaron called.

Blair broke away from Stan 5. Thinking about Nate while she was kissing him had made his lips taste much better. "I could've lasted longer," she declared, sliding off his lap. She sat down in her chair and polished off her drink. "You're next," she told Stan 5. "Truth or dare."

"Truth."

Blair tried to think of something juicy to ask him, but she only knew him in the context of Yale. "If your grandfather wasn't on the board at Yale, would you have gone to another school?"

Stan 5 cleared his throat and loosened his preppy pink-and-green-striped tie. His neck was red. "The truth?" he asked. He glanced at Blair and swiped his hand over his face. "I'm not going to Yale," he said quietly. "I didn't get in."

Nobody said anything. Blair felt bile rise in her throat. She scooted her chair back and lunged across the room toward the bathroom.

Serena smiled her mother's cool, fuck-off-and-die smile at Stanford Parris V. "I dare you to leave right now," she told him pleasantly.

Stan 5 shrugged his shoulders as if he didn't see what the big deal was. "Is she going to be okay?"

As if he really cared.

"She'll be fine," Serena assured him.

"There's a car service place around the corner," Vanessa informed him, too giddy to get what was going on.

Stan 5 stood up and straightened his tie. Serena walked him to the door. "Thanks for the pizza," he said lamely before leaving.

Vanessa and Aaron's fingers touched beneath the table. "Truth or dare?" she whispered.

"Truth," Aaron responded.

"Do you think I should grow my hair?"

Aaron leaned over and kissed her quickly on the lips. "No fucking way."

Serena went to check on Blair, expecting to find her kneeling in front of the toilet, where she'd found her countless times before. Instead, Blair was sprawled naked in the bathtub, covered in green Vitabath bubbles, a wet washcloth folded over her eyes, looking like an overworked drama queen.

"I don't know what I was thinking," she moaned, turning her head toward Serena. She was just so mad at Nate, and she wanted to go to Yale so badly, and Stan 5 had made it seem like she didn't have anything to worry about. . . .

Serena kicked off her shoes and rolled up her jeans. Then she sat on the edge of the tub and dunked her feet into the water. "I don't know either." She wiggled her pink-polished toes underneath the bubbles, daring herself to tell Blair about going to Yale next year.

Blair reached out blindly and plopped a big pouf of bubbles on Serena's cheek. "I dare you to get in with me."

Serena giggled and began to unbutton her jeans. They could talk about Yale some other time.

Back in the living room, things were just as steamy.

"Is this what you're supposed to do when you're about to graduate from high school?" Vanessa asked, helping Aaron remove his flimsy orange shirt. She kissed her way up his neck to those thin red lips she'd loved the moment she'd seen them.

"You mean make friends with the bitchiest, most high-maintenance girl in your class and then hook up with her stepbrother?" he responded honestly, then laughed. "I'm not sure." He traced his finger over the stubbly top of Vanessa's shaved head. "I guess at this point we're all ready to try new things."

Guess so!

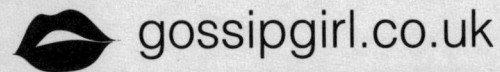gossipgirl.co.uk

topics ◀ *previous*   *next* ▶   *post a question*   reply

Disclaimer: All the real names of places, people, and events have been altered or abbreviated to protect the innocent. Namely, me.

hey people!

A star is born and she couldn't care less

Remember a few months back when a certain shaven-headed, Brooklyn dwelling, filmmaking genius won her school film contest? The prize was a trip to the Cannes Film Festival to compete for the Most Promising New Filmmaker award. Any normal girl would have been shopping for the right dress, the right shoes, the right hairstyle, the right escort, as soon as she'd found out that she'd won. She would have been counting the days. Winning the award would be like being queen for a day. Not that our filmmaking-genius friend even cares. She skipped the whole thing, and festival MC and independent filmmaker Ken Mogul had to accept the award on her behalf, calling her "the most original voice in filmmaking since Charlie Chaplin." Not necessarily a compliment, since Charlie Chaplin made *silent* films. Still, it's not every day that thousands of fabulously dressed celebrities rise to their feet to applaud you. Most of us would have wanted to be there. One thing's for sure, she's not in it for the clothes or the fame—something I find impossible to understand!

Now about her film . . .

Remember last month when that same shaven-headed filmmaker was camped out in the park, interviewing any senior kid who was willing to talk about what schools they'd gotten into or not gotten into and how their lives sucked or didn't suck? Well, guess what film won the New Filmmaker award in Cannes? Do we dare show our faces in France ever again?

Your e-mail

Q:
Dear GG,
I was wait-listed at Yale and I just got a letter from them this morning. A rejection letter. I heard no one's getting off the wait list cuz everyone who applied is going. 2 bad 4 me.
—dumdum

A:
Dear dumdum,
You are so not a dumdum for not getting in. Your guidance counselor wouldn't have let you apply if she didn't think you had a chance. I know lots of crazily smart people who didn't get in, and some dumdums who did. Anyway, does this mean everyone who's on the wait list will be hearing back this week? Guess we'll find out soon enough . . .
—GG

Q:
Dear GG,
Please tell me how to win back the heart of the boy I love. He is depressed because his father won't let him go out of the house because he is being punished for a crime. But I love him and I must see him or I will die.
—tristesse

A:
Dear tristesse,
I take it English is not your first language. Let me put it into simple terms: Maybe the boy in question isn't as into you as you are into him, n'est ce pas?
—GG

Sightings

B and **S** at the **Five and Dime** in **Williamsburg** on movie night, drinking cosmos and lip-synching along with **Audrey Hepburn** in *Charade*. **V** and **A** at the **Mousy Brown** hair salon in Williamsburg. Tell me he's not getting his head shaved to match hers! **K** and **I** making laminated No Boys Allowed signs at an Upper East Side **Kinko's**. Silly girls, don't they know that's just *asking* for trouble? A dark-haired French girl in a fringed **Prada** poncho and **Fendi** moccasins scaling the walls of

N's East-Side town house. He certainly has a penchant for crazy women. **J** and the rest of the **Raves**, on the lead singer's roof, singing her heart out in the middle of the night—*Sunday* night, that is. Guess who spent the whole weekend partying at a certain rock star's house? Now there's a girl who's in it for the fame. Is she *trying* to get her face in the papers, or does it just come naturally to her?

Now we have something to talk about in school on Monday—as if we're ever lacking for things to talk about!

P.S. Thursday night is the long-awaited Archibald Benefit Cruise to the Hamptons. Don't forget to bring your monogrammed Louis Vuitton life jacket!

You know you love me,

gossip girl

a mind is a terrible thing

Tuesday morning, as Jenny was lining her eyelids with Chanel's black liquid liner for a smoky, up-all-night effect that went perfectly with her new enormous pink Gucci sunglasses that would be the envy of Constance Billard's entire ninth grade, her dad knocked on her door and announced, "You're not going to school today, babe."

Jenny put down her eyeliner and opened the door. "What do you mean? Why not?"

Rufus was wearing a child-sized Mets baseball cap that he'd bought for Dan when he was eight. It sat like a beanie atop a nest of wild and woolly gray hair. He was also wearing blue-and-white-striped elastic-waist cotton pants that looked exactly like pajama bottoms.

"Mrs. M and I had a little talk last night," Rufus told her. *Uh-oh.*

Jenny tugged on her supershort seersucker school uniform. "How come?" she asked innocently, even though she knew perfectly well how come.

Rufus ignored her Miss I-Didn't-Do-Anything act. "She basically laid it on the line. Either you repeat ninth grade, or next year you're going to school somewhere else."

Jenny resisted hurling herself at her father and smothering him in a bear hug. She was going to boarding school! It was really happening!

Not so fast, missy.

"I'm *not* going here," Jenny insisted before the cab even stopped.

"That's what you think," her father grumbled. He paid the cabbie and opened the door. "Come, Your Tartiness. Let's take a look."

They'd pulled up in front of the Sloan Center for Bright Minds, a hippie experimental school on a flat, wide strip of boring-looking three-story buildings in Flushing, Queens. It was miles away from Manhattan and nothing like the ivy-trimmed brick buildings of the boarding school of her dreams. On the way over Rufus had shoved a Sloan Center brochure at her, and she'd thumbed through it. There was no real dress code, the lunchroom was organic and vegetarian, the students all had greasy hair and acne, and none of the teachers wore Chanel suits. In other words, Jenny hated it already.

A giant birchbark peace sign greeted them as they passed through the biodynamically grown natural oak school doors. The peace sign was hanging from the ceiling of the entryway, spinning round and round in the breeze created by the student-built watermill standing at the base of the stairs. Pure spring water cascaded down a bamboo gutter at the center of the stairs, feeding the mill.

"Our upper-schoolers built the water mill last winter," explained Calliope Trask, the school's director, at the start of their tour. "Every January we have what's called Winter Work. There are no academics, and the students focus on building something functional with their hands. The year before we had a chicken coop with twenty laying hens, right here in our gym. We had so many eggs we had an egg sale and raised the money to buy new hemp mats for our preschoolers to nap on!"

Woo-hoo!

Calliope Trask's hair hung in a gray braid down to her bottom and she was wearing a mustard-yellow-linen Eileen Fisher tank dress that did wonders for her frizzy black under-arm hair. Her legs were unshaven too, and coarse black leg hairs stuck out between the straps of her tied-at-the-ankle beige canvas Earth shoes.

"Those are wonderful sunglasses." She pointed at the gigantic pair of pink Gucci shades masking Jenny's smolder-ing brown eyes. "But at Bright Minds we don't allow designer labels or emblems on clothing or accessories of any sort."

Before Jenny could even say, "What the fuck?" Rufus had whipped the glasses off her face and stuck them in his gray sweatpants-material jacket pocket.

"That's better. Now we can see your beautiful face," Calliope trilled, as Jenny scowled hideously at her.

She followed Calliope and her father up the stairs, tempted to tell them both to take the Sloan Center for Bright Minds' hemp mats and smoke them while she ran away to the Czech Republic to live with her crazy, selfish, and neglectful mother. The Raves could do a tour of Eastern Europe and she could buy all the Gucci she wanted for half-price on the black market.

They reached the second floor and Calliope opened the door to one of the classrooms. "Our classes are mixed-age and broken up into 'bundles' named for the endangered species of the Galápagos. Jennifer, you'd be in one of the thirteen-to-fifteen-year-old bundles. I'll walk you to the area where the Giant Tortoise bundle is gathered for this morning's work and then let your student guide take over."

The floor of the classroom was covered in sand, the walls were lined with stalks of bamboo, and the ceiling was plastered with palm fronds. NO SMOKING, read a huge hand-painted sign overhead.

Jenny had never really been much of a smoker, but she was dying for a cigarette. She pulled off her white Miss Sixty cardigan to reveal the cute little Lacoste alligator marching across the left boob of her new pink shirt, given to her by Lloyd Collins of the Raves. Anything to avoid becoming a Giant Tortoise.

"Hakuna matata, Miss Calliope," a pudgy girl wearing what looked like a goatskin bikini greeted them.

"Hakuna matata, Cherisse," Calliope replied with a smile. "The Giant Tortoise bundle is exploring the country of Namibia in Africa this week," she told Jenny and Rufus, as if that explained everything. Jenny stared as the rest of the Giant Tortoises—five greasy-haired, pudgy, crooked-toothed girls and three skinny, glasses-wearing, acne-ridden boys—all wearing some form of goatskin clothing that might have been stylish if it had been designed by Stella McCartney instead of Hippies R Us. They stood in a circle, their hands joined as they sang a Namibian rain chant.

Even Rufus looked a little startled. "Do you have any data on where your graduates go to college?" he asked, sounding a lot like the parents of Jenny's Constance Billard classmates. Although he'd never have admitted it, Rufus was deadly serious about the whole college admission thing and had nearly opened all of Dan's acceptance letters before he even got home from school. He might have been an anarchist, but he was a strong believer in formal education.

Calliope frowned. "We try to keep our school as non-competitive as possible. Our students are encouraged to take some time off and explore the world. Live off the grid. Once they decide what their calling is, they may or may not seek further training."

Whatever the hell that meant.

"I hear you're an artist." Cherisse smiled at Jenny with crooked yellow teeth. "Come, I'll show you our mural. It's done entirely in buck's dung."

Rufus held Jenny's hand protectively as Cherisse led them over to a bizarre mural of elephants and zebras cavorting in the grass. Cherisse dipped her hand into a clay bowl on the floor and smeared something brown on the back of one of the elephants. Rufus shook his head tiredly and pulled Jenny over to a table in the corner of the room, where he sat down. He loved the *idea* of an alternative school, but deep down he wanted his daughter to graduate from Berkeley or Columbia, not wander around the world painting murals with deer shit.

Jenny sat down across from him and pulled a vial of Chanel Vamp nail polish out of her pink DKNY hobo bag. "So, why are we here again?" she demanded. She unscrewed the vial and began painting her nails.

Rufus readjusted his baseball cap and rubbed his bleary eyes, looking like he needed about six more hours of sleep and three more cups of coffee. "Look, Jen," he told her earnestly. "You can't just shack up with rock stars in hotels and lie to your father all the time. But I want you to be happy. What do *you* want to do?"

Jenny screwed the top back on her nail polish and put it back in her purse. She knew her dad wasn't going to like what she had to say, because he secretly adored having a house full of crazy kids to embarrass and infuriate. But the only way she was going to give up her career as a Raves groupie was if she got to go away to school, where the opportunities for adventure were limitless. Hey, he'd said it himself: He wanted her to be happy.

Across the room Calliope Trask was helping the Giant Tortoises fling buck's dung at the mural, Jackson Pollock–style.

Jenny looked up at her dear father with hopeful doe-brown eyes, her red mouth forming the shape of a heart as she murmured eight melodic words:

"Dad, may I please go to boarding school?"

a brief reminder

Dear Constance Billard Seniors,

As if you needed reminding, Senior Spa Weekend starts tomorrow! We just wanted to tell you how excited we are! And to ensure that you're dressed appropriately for the boat ride, we've had these fantastic Senior Spa Weekend long-sleeved baby tees made just for you by Three Dots. Now remember, we're the Archibalds' guests. Let's try to behave like ladies. But as soon as we get to the Coateses' estate—anything goes!

Can't wait—see you tomorrow!!!

Love,

Your classmates, Isabel and Kati.

a bird's-eye view

It was a perfect afternoon for sailing. The sun was hot and the breeze was cool. The sky was deep blue and the water was calm. Small round tables with silk tablecloths in the *Charlotte*'s colors—gold and blue—littered the deck, a heavy marble vase full of floating candles at the center of each one. In the bow of the yacht a man wearing a white tux played the double bass while a fat woman in a red muumuu crooned Nina Simone songs flawlessly. The tenants of all the finest Upper East Side addresses clutched their cocktails and chatted to one another, wearing the latest couture resortwear bought in Cannes and St. Barts. Behind them the skyline grew smaller and smaller as they coursed towards Long Island Sound and Sag Harbor.

"How *is* your son?" Misty Bass asked Mrs. Archibald, her razor-thin black eyebrows knitted in concern. A diamond cluster necklace swung heavily on her Cap d'Antibes–tanned neck as the *Charlotte* bobbed in the waves, white sails billowing. "I hear he's in trouble again. It isn't . . . *drugs*, is it?" she ventured, eager for the latest gossip.

"Nate is fine." Nate's mother bristled, the corners of her red-painted lips turned defiantly down. "He's home, studying," she lied, refusing to admit that Nate had been grounded for stealing the family boat. "Is Chuck excited about military college?"

Misty Bass poured the rest of her bourbon down her throat. Chuck had his own apartment and she'd been traveling a lot lately, so the truth was she hadn't seen him in a while. "Oh, yes," she replied vaguely. She glanced around for a cocktail server. "I do wish these glasses weren't quite so small."

"Oh, Misty!" Eleanor Waldorf cried, throwing her arms around her old friend. "You just have to see the villa in Tuscany I bought for Cyrus. It has a Web site and everything!"

On the leeward side of the boat, the guests' elder daughters were clustered in tightly packed groups, wearing their long-sleeved pink Senior Spa Weekend T-shirts, hiding from their parents, and pretending their Cokes weren't spiked with rum.

"I can't believe Nate Archibald didn't even come to his own party," Isabel Coates complained.

"That's because we said no boys allowed, stupid," Kati Farkas replied, thinking that for once she sounded smarter than her best friend.

"Don't be ridiculous," Isabel scoffed. "Boys are allowed on the boat, just not to my house for Spa Weekend."

Duh.

"Oh," Kati responded, like she'd only just gotten it.

"So vhere iizz hee?"

The two girls stared at Lexie. She went to L'École, not Constance Billard, which meant she was completely *not* invited to Senior Spa Weekend. Plus, everyone knew that her mother and Nate's mother had gone to a Catholic boarding school in France together and totally hated each other. So what was Lexie doing aboard the *Charlotte* wearing the Missoni tunic with the plunging neckline that both of them coveted but could never find, even online, her long black hair in braids like some sort of French hippie Heidi.

"Nate is grounded," Blair informed them, even though she hadn't spoken to Nate herself since their encounter at the Plaza. "He's not here." Mr. Archibald was such a hardass—of course Nate was grounded. She swayed in her three-inch beige Prada boat sandals and sucked the cherry out of her empty Coke glass, feeling extremely proud of herself for not scratching Lexie's eyes out, because the fact was she could talk about Nate without missing him at all.

Yeah, right.

Serena handed Blair another spruced-up Coke. "I'm not so sure." She was of the opinion that Nate would never miss his parents' Hamptons cruise even if he *was* grounded, and that he was hiding somewhere on the boat.

"Nate's not that creative," Blair countered, reading Serena's mind. "If he was here, we'd know."

"Nate is purrfect," Lexie drawled, toking on a joint. None of the adults onboard seemed to notice that she was getting high right on deck, perhaps because she was French and wearing Missoni.

Blair rolled her eyes and turned her back on the stupid French wretch. He might have been the only boy she would ever love, but anyone who thought Nate Archibald was perfect was a complete idiot. She watched her stepbrother Aaron scurry below deck to fetch Vanessa another rum and Diet Coke, his head newly shaved to match Vanessa's. Aaron barely knew Nate and had very definitely not been invited, but these days wherever Vanessa went, he went. If they both weren't so *un*-cute, they'd almost have been the cutest couple ever.

All of a sudden Serena felt someone tugging on the hem of her pink Spa Weekend T-shirt.

"Hey," Jenny said, standing on tiptoe to kiss her cheek. Elise was at her side, and they were both wearing pink Senior Spa Weekend T-shirts and matching oversized pink Gucci sunglasses. "You won't tell on us, will you?"

Serena had to admire Jenny's audacity. She seemed to specialize in being naughty. She put her fingers to her lips. "I won't tell," she promised, although there were only forty girls in the entire senior class, so it wasn't like no one would notice the two uninvited freshmen.

Jenny grinned and then dragged Elise belowdecks to score a bottle of champagne and Lord only knows what else. No doubt the two girls were going to get a lot naughtier as the night progressed.

"Honestly, I've given up," Dan sighed as he watched his sister and her friend disappear in a flurry of bubblegum pink. He hadn't been invited either but had tagged along with Jenny to make sure she didn't do anything too illegal. He leaned against the railing and lit a Camel, waiting patiently for Vanessa to notice him.

The familiar smell of Camel smoke wafted past her nostrils and Vanessa spun around to find Dan grinning shyly at her, his scruffy hair and loose, rust-colored corduroys billowing in the breeze. It was so unlikely that either of them would be sailing on a yacht to the Hamptons, or that she'd actually be wearing a pink T-shirt that she burst out laughing.

"What's so funny?" Dan demanded. Vanessa looked so happy right now it made him a little sad to know that it had nothing to do with him.

Aaron came back with her drink and a beer for himself. When he saw Dan and Vanessa talking he immediately handed the beer to Dan. "I'll get another one," he told them accommodatingly.

Dan couldn't believe it—even their *heads* matched.

Vanessa just stood there with a goofy smile on her face, waiting for Aaron to come back. Her happiness was infuriating, even to her. "Sorry," she apologized to Dan. "I don't know what's the matter with me."

Dan took a sip of his beer and pointed at her mouth. "Is that *lip gloss*?" he demanded with stunned amusement.

Vanessa giggled. "Nars Sticky Toffee Pudding, to be exact. I borrowed it from Blair."

They stared at one another, each waiting for the other to throw out a critical witticism about what a disgusting display of wealth and uselessness the party was. But the truth was they were both there for the same reason. Despite the fact that they had spent years trying to set themselves apart, these people were their peers, and despite all the dissing and dismissing, they actually enjoyed being included in the fun.

The Sunkist-orange ball that was the sun slid behind a horizontal wisp of cloud. The water was shiny green and flat as glass. Aaron returned with his beer and nonchalantly kissed Vanessa on the cheek. "You look pretty," he told her quietly.

Dan wondered if he had ever told Vanessa she looked pretty, but it was a little late for regrets.

"Nice job getting ditched by the band," jeered an annoyingly familiar voice. Chuck Bass was listing toward Dan from the bow of the boat, looking drunk and slightly seasick in a weird baby blue linen sailor suit with the cuffs rolled up to the knees, his white monkey clinging to his shoulder, obviously terrified of falling into the water.

Chuck was so obnoxious there was no point in getting pissed off. Besides, Dan was *overjoyed* to be a normal kid again instead of a huge rock star. He offered his hand to his monkey-toting classmate and smiled matter-of-factly. "Thanks, man."

"The Raves are so over anyway, dude," Aaron remarked. "I give them one more album and then they're gone."

"Right on." Chuck shook Dan's hand, like they'd been friends forever. "So where are you headed next year anyway, son?"

Son?

The Raves were a New York band and Dan had heard that Chuck was going to military school somewhere in northern New Jersey. It would be good to get as far away from both of them as physically possible.

"Evergreen," he announced, as if he'd always known it. "It's way out west in Washington State."

"Nice." Chuck yawned, already bored with the conversation. "Has anyone seen Serena? I heard she was dating an eighty-five-year-old Yale trustee. What a whore."

Vanessa snorted in disgust and left the boys to their own devices while she went off to find Blair and Serena. She needed a little girl time to go with her pink T-shirt.

The rest of her classmates were clustered near the bow, half-listening to the music while they clutched the rail and tried to keep from puking into the frothy waves of Long Island Sound. The sun was less intense now and the breeze had picked up. A few girls covered their arms with pashminas or royal-blue-and-gold *Charlotte* sweatshirts borrowed from the crew, but most of the passengers were too tipsy to feel the chill. Behind them the Manhattan skyline bobbed and shimmered like a miniature silver paradise inside a crystal Tiffany paperweight globe.

Serena and Blair were huddled together on a blue-and-gold-pinstriped cushion at the base of one of the masts, sharing a bottle of Heineken. "I can't believe we're about to graduate." Serena sighed and let her head fall on Blair's shoulder.

"Thank God," Blair replied unsentimentally. "I just wish I knew where the fuck I was going next year."

Serena sat up, wondering if she should take this opportunity to confess to Blair that she'd decided to go to Yale. But seeing as how they were on a boat, she didn't want to get thrown overboard.

Vanessa came over and lay down with her head in Blair's lap. "Stop talking about people, bitches," she told them, lazily closing her eyes.

"You need more lip gloss," Blair observed. She pulled a Lancôme Juicy Tube from her Earl jeans skirt pocket and carefully painted it all over Vanessa's lips.

"Thanks, Mom," Vanessa muttered, keeping her eyes closed.

Serena laughed and let her head fall back against the mast. Funny how this close to graduation all the jaggedly cut puzzle pieces that never looked like they'd fit suddenly fit together so well. Maybe she and Blair would both wind up going to Yale and rooming with each other. They'd be bridesmaids at Vanessa and Aaron's wedding; they'd meet a set of brothers and marry them, live on the same Fifth Avenue block, send their kids to the same school—friends forever.

But there was someone missing. Someone who'd always been a major piece of the puzzle in his own lovably fucked-up, cheating way.

"I wish Nate were here," Serena mused.

Blair screwed the top back on the lip gloss and began absentmindedly massaging Vanessa's pale forehead. "Sometimes I wonder if we're better off without him," she confessed. After all, wasn't Nate the cause of almost every fight the two girls had ever had?

Serena squinted her eyes and scanned the deck once more. She'd looked all over for him.

But she'd never thought to look *up*.

Way, way up, above their heads, at the very top of the mast, Nate crouched in the crow's nest, watching them. It was lonely and a little cold up there, but he'd brought along a six-pack and a few joints for company, and as soon as they docked in Sag Harbor and his parents and their friends had disbanded to their Hamptons manses, he'd climb down like Spider-Man and surprise everyone.

From up there the girls in pink T-shirts looked almost interchangeable. Even that bald chick might have been hot with a little hair. He lit a fresh joint, suddenly overcome by how much he missed them, because he loved them—he loved them all.

girls go gaga for girl-only sleepovers

In warm weather the Hamptons had their own peculiar smell of salt, new leather, sunblock, and money. Huge modern houses hunkered near white sand beaches, flanked by pools and black Mercedes SUVs. Little girls in Petit Bateau bikinis rode their scooters into town for gelato. Sleek show horses cantered elegantly along the roadside behind pristine white post-and-rail fences. Like a giant country club, the Hamptons was the type of place where only those who *belong* belong.

But of course all our girls belong.

"Head count!" Isabel Coates and Kati Farkas barked as the girls in Constance Billard's senior class stepped out of the fleet of silver town cars outside Isabel's parents' Southampton weekend home and filed into the courtyard. The house was an L-shaped one-story modern glass structure designed by Philippe Starck, with a private beach and a helicopter landing pad on the roof. In the crook of the L was a courtyard containing a floodlit pink-tiled swimming pool and a pink stucco pool house. Around the pool stood forty white plastic chaise lounges, a pink Senior Spa Weekend towel draped on the back of each one. Beside the pool, a white tent had been set up, with a buffet table covered in a pink tablecloth, and a full bar with pink Senior Spa Weekend cocktail napkins. It was almost like a wedding, except without the wedding.

Jenny Humphrey and Elise Wells skirted the line to avoid the head count and dashed across the courtyard and into the pool house.

"Hey," Rain Hoffstetter whispered shrilly to Laura Salmon. Rain and Laura were both wearing giant pink Kate Spade sun hats, and the brims of their hats kept banging against each other. "What are *they* doing here?"

"Who?" Laura Salmon demanded, squinting from underneath her hat.

"Help yourselves to cocktails and canapés!" Isabel shouted through a bullhorn, loving every minute of her boss-of-everyone role. Even though it wasn't nearly as good a school as Princeton, Isabel had decided to go to Rollins next year with Kati—much to her parents' chagrin—because Rollins had offered her a position as residence advisor in one of the freshmen women's dorms, and it would be her job to boss everyone around, including Kati, for an entire year.

"There's a steam room in the pool house. Only six at a time, please," she continued, her wide mouth pressed against the bullhorn. "There are movies in the screening room, and the pool is heated, so you can swim all night if you want to. Our high-protein, high-energy breakfast is at seven tomorrow morning, and the first Origins facial is at eight, so we'll need our beauty rest. There are queen-sized mattresses set up in every room. Three to a bed, girls—it's gonna be cozy!"

The air buzzed with the sounds of girls gathering at the bar or drifting into the house to have pillow fights on the silk-sheeted beds or raid the Origins gift bags that weren't supposed to be opened until tomorrow. A few brave girls stripped down to their underwear or changed into bathing suits and cannonballed off the diving board and into the pool, while the lazy ones gathered in Mr. Coates's screening room and sprawled on the brown leather wing-backed chairs while the opening credits of *The Great Gatsby*, starring Robert Redford and Mia Farrow, rolled past on the giant screen.

Blair, Serena, and Vanessa sat on the edge of the pool with their legs dangling into the water. "This is fun," Vanessa said in an attempt to be upbeat. She wondered how Serena and Blair kept their legs so tan. Hers were positively corpselike by comparison.

"Hey you guys!" Jenny cracked open the glass door to the pool house and beckoned to them from inside. She'd stripped down to a towel, and on her head was a white diamond-studded bathing turban, an old Hollywood-style relic Mrs. Coates wore in the pool to keep her hair from getting wet. "You gotta check out the steam room!"

Blair wasn't exactly fond of the two wannabe-senior freshmen, but she wasn't about to pass up a chance to steam off a few unwanted pounds. "Okay, but I get to wear the turban," she announced, leading the way into the pool house. She snatched the turban off Jenny's head and put it on. On Jenny it had looked ridiculous, but on Blair it was sort of regal.

Only true divas can get away with wearing turbans.

Jenny handed them each a giant white Egyptian cotton towel and the girls stripped down to nothing, all pretending not to ogle Serena's beyond-perfect body, but ogling it anyway. Secretly they each hoped to discover some hidden pocket of cellulite that she'd been hiding under her uniform all these years, but she was as slim-hipped and perfect as they'd feared.

"Supposedly Mr. Coates is a major pothead," Serena told them as she pulled off her pink T-shirt, oblivious to their stares. "That's why he only does voice-overs for commercials now instead of movies. He's smoked so much he can't remember his lines."

"I know," Jenny agreed. "Look." She unscrewed the head off an innocent-looking white marble bust of Apollo and pulled a giant bag of pot from inside it.

The three seniors stared at her. What was little Jenny Humphrey doing unscrewing the heads off of busts, anyway?

"Not that I want any," Jenny told them innocently. "Elise found it by accident."

All of a sudden Aaron's bald head bobbed past the window, and the girls squealed, hiding their naked bodies underneath their towels. It looked like he might have swum partway to get there. His clothes were wet and there was salt crusted on his cheeks.

Vanessa decided to hide from him for a while, just for fun. "Quick, get in the steam room! Now!"

Jenny threw open the door and they dodged inside. The steam room was about the size of Serena's walk-in closet, lined entirely in white tile, with two levels of steps upon which to sit. Through the steam they could just make out Elise, huddled on a white-tiled step in the corner, her body wrapped in a huge white towel and a long silver cigarette holder with a joint hanging from it dangling out of her mouth.

"Elise is getting stoned," Jenny informed them. She hoisted herself up on the lower step and handed Elise a bottle of Poland Spring. "All she wants to talk about is how she's still in love with my brother."

"Am not." Elise unscrewed the top of the bottle and guzzled the water. "Actually, I am."

"Well, he *is* cute," Serena put in, meaning it. She climbed up to the top step and sat down, crossing her ridiculously long, perfect legs. If Dan weren't so serious about everything, she would totally go out with him again. At least for a day.

"He is," Vanessa agreed, taking a seat on the step below Serena. She still felt kind of possessive of Dan despite the fact that they were broken up. If anyone could judge Dan's cuteness factor, she could.

"I guess," Blair agreed, sprawling languidly on the bottom step. She could barely remember what Dan looked like.

Jenny climbed up and sat next to Serena, hugging her knees. "Really?" she demanded, mystified.

Suddenly the door opened and Dan himself stuck his head inside. It took a while for his eyes to focus in the steamy, murky dampness. Surprise, surprise—the room was full of girls.

"Come in, come in," Vanessa croaked in her best horror movie voice. "We've been waiting for you."

Dan grinned sheepishly and bit his lower lip. He was wearing red swim trunks and nothing else and his hair was wet. Goosebumps stood out all over his pale arms. "Is my sister here?"

"Yes, loser, and Elise is here too," Jenny replied through the steam. "She's still in love with you."

"We're *all* in love with you," Serena proclaimed.

Dan sat down on the white-tiled step next to a prone girl in a white diamond-studded turban.

"I'm not in love with you," the girl told him. "I don't even know you."

Well, that's a relief.

The door opened again and Aaron poked his head inside. "'Nessa?" he called sweetly, his rosy cheeks all sprinkled with sand.

"Over here," Vanessa answered through a cloud of steam.

"Come and join our sweatfest. Just don't look at all the other naked girls."

Aaron tiptoed across the tile in his maroon Harvard T-shirt and sand-spattered army green pants and sat down on Vanessa's lap. Jenny reached out and turned the dial to raise the temperature of the steam.

As if it needed to be raised.

"Wow. This *is* fun," Serena observed. She wiped the sweat from her upper lip and slid to her feet. "I have to pee. Does anyone want anything?"

"Yeah, but there's nothing *you* can do about it," Blair replied smugly.

She'd been trying to convince herself that this girls-only bonding thing was totally fine with her, but now that there were all these guys around, her true feelings had risen to the surface. She wanted *her* boyfriend to appear out of the steam and surprise her. He'd slip a diamond ring on her finger, cover her shoulders with a creamy cashmere cape, and whisk her off in his pearl gray convertible Jag to a private, moonlit beach where he would beg her forgiveness with every kiss. At dawn, his sailboat would float up out of the mist to whisk them away to faraway lands, and they'd spend the rest of their lives having adventures and making love. She wanted the true Hollywood ending.

Hence the turban.

Serena pushed the steam room door open. Cold air bathed her face.

"Shit, Blair," she heard Aaron say behind her. "I can't believe I forgot. I have something for you."

And what might that be?

if you're too stoned to find the one you love, love the one you're with

The steam room door closed behind her and Serena padded across the pool house in search of the bathroom. For a pool house, it was really quite big. It contained a Ping-Pong table, two king-sized ivory leather sleeper sofas, and a fish tank with a live barracuda in it. Not to mention the steam room and the bathroom that had to be around here somewhere.

Someone had clearly been into Mr. Coates's pot stash, because Apollo's head was rolling around underneath the Ping-Pong table like an oversized Ping-Pong ball. Next to the fish tank was a white door with a picture of a little blue boy and a little pink girl holding hands decoupaged onto it. Serena pushed it open.

Inside, the bathroom was decorated in gold leaf and had one of those weird low sinks you always see in European hotels but that no one ever uses.

Because they're for washing your butt, which is beyond gross?

The shower curtain was made of clear plastic decorated with gold stars. Behind it, sitting inside the tub with Mr. Coates's pot stash cradled in his lap, his clothes damp with seawater, and his eyes all red and sleepy, was Nate Archibald—the famously missing Nate. Serena pulled the shower curtain aside and climbed inside the tub, clutching her towel around her.

"Natie? What are you doing here? Why weren't you on the boat?"

Nate grinned foolishly. Serena was naked except for a white towel wrapped around her torso. It was impossible not to smile at her; she looked like a Greek goddess. Her forehead was damp, and her blond hair was matted with sweat, but she was still gorgeous. Beyond gorgeous.

She pulled her hair up on top of her head and fanned her face. "God, I'm hot."

Of course, Nate was thinking the same thing.

"I'm not supposed to be here," Nate confided idiotically. "The sign said, NO BOYS ALLOWED."

Serena picked up a clear glass bottle of Clarins bath gel from the edge of the tub and examined it. Aqua was the first ingredient. Didn't that mean water? she wondered. Why didn't they just say so? She put the bottle down again. "That's okay. Blair's stepbrother is here. And Dan Humphrey. I didn't think the no-boys policy would work."

Nate's eyes hadn't left her face. Tiny beads of water studded her blond-tipped eyelashes. God, she was pretty. He'd come here looking for Blair, but Serena was right there in front of him, wearing only a *towel*.

"I've decided to go to Yale next year," Serena blurted out, brushing the damp tendrils of blond hair away from her face. "I haven't told Blair yet because I don't want her to be mad in case she doesn't get in. But that's where I've decided to go."

Nate nodded. It was funny how Serena's face and even her voice were sort of delicate but her body wasn't delicate at all. It was long and sinewy and strong, like a marathon runner's.

"I'm going there too," he told her giddily, his voice cracking. "I already sent them my deposit."

Serena grinned. "We're both going to Yale!"

Nate leaned toward her and clasped the tops of her bare, damp arms in his hands. He pressed his nose into her long, fair hair. She smelled sweet and warm, like summer. "Mmm," he murmured, and kissed her soft, warm neck, tasting the signature patchouli-scented essential oil mixture she always wore.

Hello? Wrong-girl alert!

Serena grinned as his lips traveled up her neck to her lips. "What are you doing?" she murmured without pushing him away. It had been a while since she'd been kissed, and it felt nice. Of course it was kind of wrong, but it wasn't like she and Nate hadn't kissed before, and somehow knowing that they were going to be together next year made it seem okay.

She closed her eyes and gave herself up to the kiss. Her towel fell away, and somehow Nate's damp gray T-shirt seemed to fall away too.

It was the end of the year, graduation was fast approaching—there was nothing wrong with a little celebratory hookup between two best friends.

Yeah, but what about their *other* best friend?

nobody does it better

Blair was dripping with sweat and badly in need of a vodka tonic. She hitched up her towel. "What is it?" she asked Aaron impatiently.

Aaron stood up and patted his army shorts pockets. "I've got it," he explained. "At least I hope it's still there." He fumbled around for a moment and then produced what looked like a damp white envelope.

Blair squeezed her eyes shut and then opened them again. She was pretty sure she knew what the enveloped contained. "And you've had that for exactly how long?" she demanded furiously before snatching it out of his hand.

Aaron shrugged innocently. "It just came this morning."

Even through the steam Blair could see the familiar royal blue of Yale's insignia printed in the upper-left-hand corner of the envelope. The dampness made the envelope disintegrate as she attempted to pry it open with shaking, impatient hands. "Fuck it," she breathed and ripped it open with her teeth.

A single, flimsy, bitten-into piece of paper was folded up inside. Her life had been hanging in the balance for months now. It was hard to believe it all depended on *this*.

The others waited with respectful silence.

Dear Blair Waldorf,

After much consideration we are happy to offer you a place at Yale University this coming fall. . . .

Blair clutched the piece of paper to her chest and tore out of the steam room. "Serena!" she shrieked, dashing across the pool house and heading straight for the bathroom. She yanked open the door, expecting to see her friend perched innocently on the toilet.

Inside, a tangle of familiar, gorgeous, naked limbs greeted her from the bathtub. Nate and Serena blinked stupidly up at her, their golden heads only inches apart.

"We were celebrating," Serena stammered. She climbed out of the tub, her towel clutched ineffectually around her naked body, and pointed at the soggy piece of paper in Blair's hand. "What's that?" she asked in a desperate attempt to change the subject.

Blair felt like washing out Serena's perfectly angelic mouth in the Coateses' stupid bidet. "Yale accepted me. Finally." She narrowed her eyes. "As if you cared."

Nate staggered to his feet, spilling the giant bag of pot all over the bathtub and ripping the shower curtain off the rail as he tried to find his balance. Infuriating as it was, he was still as handsome as ever. His golden brown hair was wavy from the wind and salt air, and his cheeks were flushed from sun and pot and kissing Serena. And his bare chest—it made Blair feel ill to look at it.

"Hey, you know, that's what we were just talking about," he fumbled, his tongue heavy with a mixture of pot, confusion, and guilt. "Me and Serena, and now you too. We're all going to Yale—all three of us!"

Whoopee!

"Thanks for telling me," Blair snapped. She'd imagined

sharing a celebratory bottle of champagne with Serena on the Coateses' private beach. Then she'd give in and call Nate's cell and he'd kidnap her from the party and make wild love to her on some other beach.

So much for her imagination.

Nate was still standing in the bathtub, his bare feet sprinkled with pot. She reached out and turned the shower nozzle on full blast, raining freezing cold water all over his head. Then she yanked off Serena's towel and tucked it under her arm, slamming the door in their lying, cheating faces as she left the bathroom.

Lexique or whatever the fuck her name was drifted into the pool house in her annoying Missoni tunic, her braids bouncing against her braless breasts, just as Blair was headed out the door. "He's in der, yes? My lover, my Nate?"

Blair bared her teeth with evil satisfaction. "Oh, yes. He's waiting for you in the bathroom," she told the stupid French bitch, slamming the pool house door behind her and making a beeline for the poolside bar.

There seemed to be more guys under the tent than girls. Damian, Lloyd, and Marc from the Raves were mingling with the Constance Billard seniors, handing out cigars and copies of their new single, "Twisted Little Sister," starring none other than Jenny Humphrey on vocals. The girls had taken off their T-shirts and were all wearing bright, pastel-colored bikini tops, looking like the extras in one of those old Elvis beach movies.

Chuck Bass was trying to talk Rain Hoffstetter, Laura Salmon, Kati Farkas, and Isabel Coates into joining him at military school. "It doesn't really matter where you go to school. What matters is how much fun you have," Blair heard him say. "Just think how fabulous it would be if we were all together!"

Blair went over to the bar, grabbed a half-full bottle of Absolut, and carried it over to the pool.

"Hey, no glass around the pool!" Isabel shouted through her bullhorn.

Blair ignored her and climbed up the ladder to the high-dive. She let her towel drop, and padded out to the end of the diving board.

A naked diva in a diamond-studded turban, swigging her favorite beverage.

Ignoring the shocked murmurs of her classmates and the delighted jeers of the guys beneath the tent, Blair took a moment to rewind. She and Nate were obviously over—again, and so were she and Serena—again. She was living in Brooklyn of all places, with Vanessa, a shaven-headed girl she'd never spoken to until about a week ago. And she was finally, finally into Yale.

Most of her life had been an endless loop of repetition, filled with the same people, parties, and predictability. Even her dreams had been predictable, and she liked it like that. Now she wasn't sure what to expect.

She lifted the bottle to her lips and took a giant swig before setting it carefully down on the diving board. Then she raised her arms up straight as arrows, stood on tiptoe, and dove in. Holding her breath, she glided beneath the blue-green water, delighting in the silence. Behind her, the diamond-studded turban bobbed to the surface.

When she really thought about it, this whole year had been a series of highs and lows, with more lows than highs. But so what if her life wasn't turning out the way she'd imagined it in the movie in her head, and her entire supporting cast had turned out to be assholes? She was about to move the film to a completely new location and could hire an entirely new cast. And nobody knew how to steal the show better than Blair did.

Her dark head broke the surface with a dramatic, noisy splash. The others stared, tittering from underneath the tent, but Blair paid them no mind. Floating on her back, she chanted a goofy little rhyme to cheer herself up.

"Two, four, six, eight, only nineteen days till I graduate!"

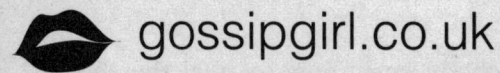

gossipgirl.co.uk

hey people!

Senior Spa Weekend = senior sick weekend

Turns out nearly everyone who used the Coateses' steam room or the pool or borrowed a towel from someone who used the steam room or the pool woke up with a disgusting, itchy, oozy, rash all over their face. The Origins spa people were sent home immediately and a serious dermo was called in for damage control. Curiously, our bathing beauty **B** had nary a mark on her face. The dermo explained that she was probably immune but could be a carrier. Curiouser still, the rash looked exactly like the rash on a certain baby that **B** had exposed herself to, despite her family's efforts to keep the baby quarantined. Well, at least everyone had a good excuse for missing school on Friday! And with ninety-nine percent of the senior class in quarantine, Constance Billard had no choice but to give the seniors the entire week off.

B took the opportunity to fly to Paris to see her dad and bumped into her mother in Chanel on the Left Bank. Apparently her mom was trying to buy the whole company as a gift to **B** for finally getting into Yale. As the company was not for sale, **B** settled for four skirts, six pairs of sling-backs, and three evening clutches—how sensible of her! **V** would have gone with her, but she was in quarantine, poor thing. Not that she didn't have fun playing doctor with her new bf. And what about **S** and **N**? He was seen on his way to her Fifth Avenue penthouse on the pretense of borrowing her rash-soothing skin cream, but methinks he might have enjoyed a little game of doctor too.

What everyone can look forward to as soon as their skin clears up

Insane rooftop graduation parties.

Shopping for white graduation dresses that pass the no-cleavage rule but don't make us look like fat bridesmaids.

Shopping for escorts to graduation parties who won't get too drunk and throw up all over our gorgeous new dresses.

Shopping for the perfect pair of white heels to wear with our graduation dresses. Not too high, though—we have to march into graduation in size order, and no one wants to be last.

Making a wish list of graduation gifts. Can you spell *C-A-R*, anyone?

Getting everything on our wish lists. Vroom, vroom, vroom!

Graduation!!!!

Some unfinished business

Are **S** and **N** a couple? If not, what exactly *are* they?

Will **B** ever speak to them again? Will she get revenge?

Will **B** and **V** continue to cohabitate now that **A** is always hanging around?

Will **D** continue to be a normal kid—sort of? Will he meet a normal girl?

Will **J** get into boarding school? Will she stay out of trouble until she gets there?

Will we all actually graduate?!

Guess who will have all the answers?

You know you love me,

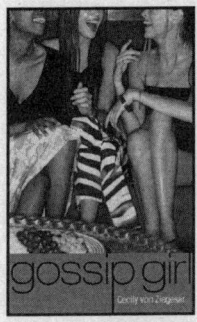